SUGAR SKULLS
AND SPECTERS

LATTES AND LEVITATION - BOOK 5

CHRISTINE POPE

Dark Valentine Press

SUGAR SKULLS AND SPECTERS

Copyright © 2023 by Christine Pope

ISBN: 978-1-946435-67-5

Published by Dark Valentine Press

Cover design by Romancepremades.com.

Ebook formatting by Indie Author Services

Don't miss out on any of Christine's new releases—sign up for her newsletter today!

CHAPTER 1

Skull Candy

"You're sure you'll be able to make all the sugar skulls, Skye?" Carrie Thomas asked me. She was the mayor's assistant—new to her post, since her predecessor was currently in prison for being an accessory to murdering Tom Gallegos, the former mayor—and always seemed a little anxious, no matter how smoothly things might be going.

In this case, I thought her obvious nerves might be somewhat warranted. My hometown of Las Vegas, New Mexico, would be hosting its first official Day of the Dead celebration in less than a week, and Carrie was in charge of making sure it went off without a hitch. Like most other civic celebrations in Las Vegas, the event was going to be held in Plaza Park, just down the street from my coffee shop and right across from the town's historic Plaza Hotel.

I couldn't help wondering what any of the hotel's remaining resident ghosts would think of the observance. Day of the Dead festivals had been getting more and more mainstream the past few years, with many people finding their own comfort in the colorful holiday that honored beloved family members and friends who'd passed on, so that's why I wasn't too surprised that Carrie had come up with the idea to have one here in Las Vegas as well. Our town had a fairly large Hispanic population, some of whom were acting as her advisors so she wouldn't make any awkward cultural missteps.

But none of them knew how to make the sugar skulls that were such an important part of the observance...*El Dío de los Muertos* was more of a tradition in the parts of our state that bordered Mexico itself...which was why Carrie had come to see me. True, my real talents lay in making delectable muffins and croissants—along with the fancy pastries I'd added to my inventory earlier this year—but obviously, she thought that if I could pull off napoleons and eclairs, then I should be able to produce a decent batch of sugar skulls.

"Absolutely," I said stoutly. "I've been reading up on the process, and I've watched a bunch of how-to videos on YouTube. It's really not that hard, especially since you don't need me to decorate all of them. That'll save a lot of time."

Part of Carrie's plan for the Day of the Dead festival was to have a booth where kids could paint their own sugar skulls with various colors of icing, which meant half of the two hundred or so skulls I would be making could be left plain. I thought it was a great idea, both because the kids would probably have a lot of fun with the project, and also because I hadn't really been looking forward to coming up with unique designs for two hundred sugary craniums.

She let out a relieved breath. At thirty-five, she was five years older than me, and almost my exact opposite in looks, being blonde and blue-eyed and just a little plump. However, we were both Las Vegas natives, although I'd never really been acquainted with her in school because of our age difference. I did know that she had two little girls, ten and seven, and that on top of running the mayor's office, she was also active in the local PTA.

No wonder she looked so wrung out most of the time.

Privately, I'd worried that she might have bitten off more than she could chew with the Day of the Dead festival, although I would never have uttered those doubting words out loud. So far, though, everything seemed to be going smoothly enough, with vendors and performers and musicians lined up for the event, and the weather—which could get kind of iffy toward the end of October—cooperating nicely, with sunny days and temperatures well above our usual average of the low fifties.

Now if this lovely run of pleasant weather would only last through Saturday. Because the actual Day of the Dead—November first through the second—fell in the middle of the week, the festival itself was being held on Saturday, the fourth. Also, with Halloween tomorrow, the mild temperatures were a definite blessing. I had plenty of recollections of my grandmother, who'd raised me, insisting on me wearing a sweater or jacket over my costume, which kind of ruined whatever effect I'd been going for.

"Then it sounds like it's all going to work out just fine," Carrie said. Her phone beeped from inside her purse, and she pulled it out, glanced down at the screen, and shook her head. "Well, I need to get going. The mayor needs me."

"Do you want a coffee for the road?" I asked her, even as I thought she probably didn't need any more caffeine.

"No, I'm fine," she answered at once, which was how I'd thought she'd respond. "I'll check in again on Wednesday."

I nodded, and didn't bother to protest that I had everything handled and she really didn't need to keep checking on me. Carrie thought that micromanaging every little detail was part of her job, and nothing I said was going to change her mind.

Instead, I waved as she headed out, then noticed that my best friend—and my one and only employee—Deanne had just emerged from our combination kitchen/stockroom at the back of the coffee shop.

Her expression was disapproving. Like Carrie, Deanne was blonde and blue-eyed, but the resemblance stopped there, since Deanne was slim and effortlessly pretty, and never looked too worried about anything. "I still don't think you should have signed up to make all those sugar skulls," she said.

"It's fine," I assured her. "If I thought it would be too much, I would have said no. But the molds arrived today, and the rest of the supplies will be here tomorrow. In fact," I added, knowing that I probably wore an impish smile, "the whole process is easy enough that I'll bet you can do a bunch, too."

One eyebrow lifted. "I don't remember signing up for that."

"Hey, it's a Levitation Latte project," I said. "That means we both need to pitch in."

Deanne let out a small huff of a breath, but I noticed she didn't bother to continue the argument. Maybe she was thinking it over and realizing that helping pour liquid sugar into a bunch of molds would be a lot easier than taking over the job of baking muffins or something. Even after working with me for almost four years, she still hadn't become much of a baker. Yes, if I made the batter ahead of time and all she had to do was pour it into the muffin tins and put them in the oven, she could manage that much, but asking her to do anything more complicated than that was a recipe for disaster.

So to speak.

"Anyway," I went on, "I won't even need to start making them until Wednesday at the earliest, so it's not like I'm going to chain you to the stove on Halloween or something."

She grinned. "Well, even if you did, it's not like I'd be missing much except handing out candy."

True enough. Because Halloween fell on a Tuesday this year, everyone had done most of their partying the weekend before. In fact, my boyfriend Max—Max Sullivan, Hollywood superstar, and the guy I'd had a crush on for most of my life—had thrown another of his blowout Halloween bashes on Saturday night. Even though we'd been officially a couple since early June, it had still felt kind of unreal to attend the party at his side, to know that everyone there saw us together and didn't think anything was particularly strange about the situation.

Whereas I still had the urge to pinch myself

from time to time, usually when Max came to pick me up for dinner and I saw him striding along the front walk, looking gorgeous as ever and like someone who should have been dating someone much more fabulous than Skye O'Malley, owner of the local coffee shop.

Maybe after enough time elapsed, I'd finally be able to acknowledge the reality of the situation. It definitely didn't seem as if Max was going anywhere, that was for sure.

Oh, it had been rough when he'd left at the end of June to shoot an action picture with locations all over the world, including Iceland and Dubai, but at least that production—unlike the one that had preceded it—had remained on schedule, and he'd been back in the middle of August as planned.

Even so, that had been probably the longest eight weeks of my life, and I was very, very glad that he didn't have another film lined up until late January. I knew he often shot three movies in the space of a year, but I hadn't quite gotten the nerve to ask him whether he'd cut back on my account. Yes, I much preferred having him with me here in Las Vegas, but I also didn't want to be the reason why he didn't seem to be working as much as he used to.

"And you're sure you don't want to come over to my place for Halloween?" I asked Deanne then, but she only shook her head.

"Nope—we've got way too many little kids in our neighborhood for Mike and me not to be there to hand out candy," she said. "It's fine—we all got our Halloween on Saturday night, anyway."

That was true. Max definitely knew how to throw a party, and there had probably been close to two hundred people there for his Halloween get-together. Luckily, his house was large, and because the weather had been so mild, a lot of his guests had spilled out onto the property's equally expansive patios.

And I wouldn't be spending Halloween itself alone, despite Deanne and Mike staying at home, because Max would be over at my place, helping me greet all the trick-or-treaters. We'd decided that was the best thing to do, because his ranch was located way at the eastern edge of town on a private lane, and wasn't exactly the kind of place where you could expect many kids looking for treats.

Whereas mine was an established neighborhood of old houses, with wide sidewalks and plenty of opportunities to get lots of candy, and since I always made caramel apples, I often had people driving in from other parts of town so they could get something a lot more special than some fun-size candy bars bought at the local Walmart.

"Okay," I said. I'd already guessed that Deanne would want to stay home, but I figured I'd better make sure. "Then I guess we'd better get ready for the lunch rush."

———

Max and I had fallen into a pattern of alternating where we spent our evenings, and since he was coming over tomorrow for Halloween, I headed out to his ranch once I'd locked up the shop for the day. I didn't always spend the night, mostly because I had to be up before the crack of dawn so I could get to the coffee shop and make that morning's batches of muffins and pastries before we opened at seven o'clock, but we still got to have plenty of quality time together.

Besides, Lou, one of Max's bodyguards, was a gourmet cook, and it was always nice to eat a meal that I didn't have to prepare myself. Don't get me wrong—I loved to cook...Max sometimes called me his "kitchen witch"—but on the other hand, having a break every once in a while was something to savor.

This evening, Al, the other half of Max's security detail, was watching the gate when I approached in my light blue Subaru Crosstrek. As usual, Al waved me in without hesitation, and I waved and smiled as I drove past him. Max had given me a key to his house, just as I'd given him a key to mine, although there didn't seem to be much point in my having that key, not when someone was always watching the road to the ranch.

But I'd appreciated the gesture all the same, knowing that Max had done so because he wanted me to know that he trusted me with his property, and that ours definitely wasn't a casual relationship.

Not that I'd ever thought any such thing, not since that first time we'd kissed and we'd both realized this was something real, something the two of us had been dancing around for much longer than necessary. Ever since then, we'd been pretty much inseparable, except for when I was at work or he was off shooting a movie.

Once or twice, Deanne had sent me some pretty broad hints about Max needing to make things extra real by putting a ring on it, but I'd only shaken my head. Yes, I knew things were serious between us, and yet I also realized that we'd only been dating for barely five months.

And okay, we'd known each other since we were little kids, but still.

He was waiting at the door as I drove up—something he always did, since Al would call him to let him know I'd passed the gate and would be there shortly. And, as always, he bent and gave me a vigorous kiss, the kind that never failed to thrill me to the very tips of my toes.

"How was work?" he asked, after he stepped back so he could close the door behind him.

"Fine," I replied, knowing I sounded a little breathless from the kiss, "the usual. Although Deanne got a little miffed when I suggested she should help me with all those sugar skulls."

That comment made him grin, lighting up his amazing blue eyes. Max's smiles had always been incandescent, something that seemed to beam right down from a movie screen and be intended only for you.

Or maybe I just saw it that way because I'd been in love with him, quietly, desperately, for most of my life.

Not that I had any need to be desperate anymore. All those girlish dreams had come true, and I was now with the only man I'd ever loved.

"Hey, I told you I'd help, too," he said in mock-wounded tones. "Or don't you trust me in the kitchen?"

"Of course I do," I replied serenely, since I knew he was teasing me just a little. "But do you really want to spend hours pouring molten sugar into a bunch of skull molds?"

"Sure," he said at once, just as I'd thought he would. "It sounds like fun."

That was just another thing I loved about Max —his apparently boundless enthusiasm for anything novel, anything that required him to learn something new. I'd been a little worried that eventually he'd tire of living in quiet Las Vegas, New Mexico, and would want to head back to L.A., and return to his fast-paced life in that glamorous city. Because we hadn't visited there yet, I couldn't quite help viewing Los Angeles as a kind of gorgeous ex-girlfriend, one who might want to intrude on his life at the worst moment.

Those fears had proved groundless, though. True, he'd been amusing himself by taking flying lessons at the general-aviation airport that was only a few minutes from his ranch, and also by having Lou teach him to cook, so it wasn't as though he'd had much time to get truly bored. And that didn't count our horseback rides, or our occasional trips to Santa Fe and Taos.

Well, when I looked at it that way, I supposed I didn't have to worry too much about Max not finding enough activities to fill his time.

"Then come in after we close on Wednesday," I told him. "That'll give me time to hunt up an extra-large apron for you."

He winked at me, as I had a feeling he would, and we headed into the dining room. Wonderful aromas drifted in from the kitchen, telling me Lou had put together another one of his amazing pizzas for us.

Sure enough, that evening we were treated to a concoction of prosciutto and goat cheese and drizzles of spicy honey, just the perfect thing for a mild October day that still had a bit of bite to it after the sun went down. Max and I talked about the upcoming Day of the Dead festival, of our plans to go to Taos for the Veterans Day weekend. I generally closed the coffee shop on federal holidays like that, just because so many of my customers would have the day off as well, and there usually wasn't much point in staying open.

"But you're sure you don't want to dress up when we hand out candy tomorrow night?" he asked as our meal wound to a close.

I tried not to smile. For someone who spent a sizeable chunk of his life in wardrobe when he was shooting a film, that man of mine still loved wearing costumes.

"We wore our Gomez and Morticia costumes on Saturday night," I pointed out. Those costumes had been gorgeous, like something right off a movie set, and I hadn't wanted to ask what they must have set him back. "And when I get home from work tomorrow, I'm going to be making caramel apples like a madwoman. I don't think I'm going to have time to change before the littlest trick-or-treaters start showing up."

And okay, I'd already made several batches of the apples and wrapped them in festive cellophane with orange and black curly ribbon, but I knew I still had to do a lot more on the day of.

Being Max, he took this information in stride. "Oh, right," he said. "Do you need help with the apples?"

"Absolutely," I said. "You can wrap them while I dip. That way, we'll be finished a lot quicker."

With that plan agreed on...and the last sips of our wine and bites of pizza consumed...we both got up from our seats and cleared the table. Then Max's hand stole in mine, and he bent down to give me a thrilling kiss on the back of my neck, one that sent shivers down my spine as he lifted my heavy dark hair out of the way.

"Can you stay a while longer?" he asked in a murmur.

Since most of our evenings together ended this way, I didn't even hesitate.

"Absolutely," I said.

CHAPTER 2

Trick or Treat

Halloween was always kind of a mixed bag at the shop. Deanne and I didn't really dress up, although she had a pair of cat ears she usually donned for the occasion, while I settled for a necklace of blinking candy-corn LED lights over my usual black T-shirt. Our customers, on the other hand, came in wearing everything from their normal business attire to full-on vampire and clown and zombie costumes.

In fact, Kyle Isaacs, one of the local deputies—and an ex-boyfriend of mine—came in wearing such a scarily accurate Pennywise from *It* that Deanne almost told him to turn around and get the hell out.

"I can't believe you're wearing that to work," she said severely. "It's *awful.*"

He removed the horrible rubber mask,

revealing what could only be described as a shit-eating grin. "I'm doing the overnight shift today," he said. "So I'm not on duty until eight."

Which sort of begged the question why he'd come into the coffee shop now, since it was his habit to drop by in the middle of his morning shift so he could fortify himself with a cup of coffee and a muffin or maybe a croissant.

Then again, I guessed exactly why he'd showed up this morning—he wanted to give Deanne and me a good scare.

But I figured I should cut him some slack, mostly because I thought it probably wasn't a lot of fun to have to work on Halloween. Even when the holiday fell on a weeknight, some people could get kind of out of control.

"Are you working at the Day of the Dead festival?" I asked, and Kyle nodded.

"Yeah, Chief DeVargas wants as many of us as she can spare from patrol duty, just to make sure everything stays nice and quiet."

On the surface, one wouldn't have thought those sorts of precautions were necessary in sleepy little Las Vegas. However, none of us could forget that the former mayor had been murdered by his very own brother at last year's harvest festival, so I had a feeling the police chief was just being super vigilant to make sure nothing like that happened this go-'round.

True, this year's harvest celebration had gone off without a hitch—it was usually held in the middle of October—so it looked as if Chief De Vargas didn't have much to worry about.

I hoped.

"But I don't mind," Kyle went on. "It sounds like it's going to be fun, and I don't expect there to be any problems."

Because the Day of the Dead event was meant to honor the souls of those who had passed, it probably would be fairly low-key, not some crazy drunken bacchanalia. Just like at the harvest festival, no alcohol was being sold at the vendors' booths...although I knew that still wouldn't stop some people from boozing it up before they went over to see the exhibits and performers, or bringing along a handy flask so they could spike the sodas they bought on site.

Well, hopefully, the increased police presence would be a sign that the attendees needed to behave themselves, no matter what.

We talked a little more about the dancers who would perform and the various bands that would take shifts at the bandstand—not Kyle's country-rock group, unfortunately, since he would be on duty that night—and then he headed out, saying he wanted to wander and see who else he could scare silly.

After he left, Deanne sent a significant glance in my direction. "He seemed okay."

"Why wouldn't he be?" I asked, even though I knew exactly what she was talking about.

She put her hands on her hips. Unlike me—I rarely bothered with those kinds of things, since I was almost always doing something in the kitchen—she wore a fun Halloween-themed manicure in orange and black, with spiderwebs painted on the nails of both ring fingers. "Because of you and Max."

I caught myself before I rolled my eyes. "Deanne, Max and I have been going out for months now. Kyle's had plenty of time to get used to us being together."

Which was true. Sure, at first, he hadn't been very happy...to put it mildly...but as time wore on and it became pretty clear that Max's and my relationship wasn't some flash in the pan, Kyle seemed to become resigned to the situation. There had never been even the remotest chance of the two of us getting back together, and now that I was obviously together with Max Sullivan, Kyle had at last put that pipe dream aside.

If only I could have thought of someone to fix him up with.

But the dating pool in Las Vegas wasn't exactly what you could call large, and he hadn't seemed interested in any of the women our age who were still single and hadn't decided to settle down and get married. Honestly, beyond buying him an eHarmony membership or secretly downloading the Tinder app to his phone, I didn't know what I was supposed to do.

"Still," Deanne said, "it's nice that he's accepting you being with Max. Back when you two first got together, I saw Kyle practically staring daggers at him when Max came in to see you."

"He did?" I responded, startled. True, back then I'd been so moony about being with Max that I might not have noticed my ex-boyfriend's response to the situation, but I really didn't want to think I'd been quite *that* oblivious.

"Oh, you were in the back that time," Deanne told me. "So you wouldn't have even seen it. Still, Kyle was pretty hostile. I'm just glad to see how much he's mellowed out."

No wonder I hadn't noticed anything. I wasn't sure why Deanne hadn't mentioned the incident to me at the time, but maybe she'd decided it was better to keep quiet and hope Kyle would settle into the reality of Max and me as time went on.

Which seemed to be pretty much exactly what had happened, so I supposed she'd been wise in not saying anything.

"Me too," I said, and left it at that.

Business was brisk the rest of the day, busier than a normal Tuesday. I'd found it was often like that on Halloween, that, rather than saving their sugar quota for whatever treats they'd be consuming that night, a lot of people seemed to think the entire day was open season for eating whatever they felt like.

And that was fine by me. Not just because I liked those days when we were in the black before we even hit ten o'clock in the morning, but because a nice, steady flow of customers made the time pass by that much more quickly.

Which meant three-thirty came around faster than I'd expected, and Deanne and I said our goodbyes and headed for our respective homes after we locked up the shop and turned on the alarm. I'd barely pulled into the driveway when I saw Max's black Bronco come gliding up to the curb.

Smiling to myself—I loved that he was so eager to see me even though we'd been a couple for almost five months by now—I clicked the remote for the garage door opener and drove inside. I'd finally bit the bullet a month earlier and gotten the new garage door and its accompanying opener installed, telling myself I had to do it eventually, and better to get it handled before winter arrived. Wanting to avoid trudging through the snow to open the old door manually had been a great motivator.

Max met me at the back door and leaned down

for a hello kiss. I noticed he was carrying a couple of grocery bags, and I sent them a questioning look.

"What're those?"

"Oh," he replied, with one of his patented Max Sullivan smiles, "I figured I should probably bring some backup, just in case."

He opened one of the bags a little, just enough to show me it held several packages of fun-size Snickers and Twix and other small candy bars.

I sent him some serious side-eye at that. "We're not going to need those."

"Maybe not," he replied easily as I unlocked the back door. "But I just thought it might help in case you ran out of caramel apples."

"Not likely," I told him, then headed inside the kitchen, Max right behind me. "I've been doing caramel apples for Halloween for years. I know how many I need to make."

"Probably," he said, his tone still cheerful. "This is just insurance. And if we don't end up using them, I'll donate them to the youth center or the police station or something."

Slightly mollified, I just shrugged, and headed to the pantry to fetch the bags of apples I'd bought a few days earlier and had already cleaned of wax, along with all the ingredients I needed for the caramel itself—brown sugar, heavy cream, corn syrup, butter. By now, Max knew enough to stay out of the way while I was getting prepped, so he stood off to one side, clearly waiting for me to give the order to have him come help when I was ready.

Because I'd done this what felt like a million times, it didn't take long for me to get the caramel going and lay out all the cookie sheets—carefully covered in wax paper—where we'd set the apples down after I was done dipping them.

"You can dip," I told Max. "That's the most fun part."

From the way his expression brightened, you'd have thought I'd told him I was going to buy him a pony for Christmas. He came right over to the stove, and we got a kind of assembly line going, with me inserting the sticks in the apples and then handing them over to Max, who got the hang of the process quickly enough that we soon had dozens of apples cooling on their various baking sheets.

"Once they've cooled down, we can wrap them," I said.

"How long will that take?"

"About a half hour or so. We'll have them ready in plenty of time."

Which proved to be the case, because we had about six dozen apples wrapped and ready to go by the time six o'clock rolled around. That was the unofficial start time for trick-or-treating in my neighborhood, and, sure enough, the doorbell rang at promptly 6:01.

We'd moved most of the trays to either the coffee table or the dining room table so we wouldn't have to travel far to grab another cookie sheet when one was emptied. I'd told Max he could do the honors if he wanted to, so he was the one who answered the door.

Standing outside were the O'Connors, a family who'd moved in down the street about six months earlier. They had a three-year-old and a baby who was just eleven months, and who was wearing the cutest little T-Rex costume while she sat in her stroller.

Leigh O'Connor was about my age, maybe a year or so older, and I couldn't help noticing the way her smile froze as she realized exactly who was handing over a cellophane-wrapped caramel apple to her three-year-old.

"Happy Halloween!" Max said, and she stammered something in response before all but fleeing down the porch steps, leaving her husband to maneuver the stroller back to the front walk.

"You charmer, you," I joked as he shut the door.

Max grinned. "I get the feeling she wasn't expecting to see me here."

"Probably not," I replied with a smile of my own. Because the O'Connors were new to Las Vegas, I wasn't sure whether they'd really tapped into the town's grapevine or not. Otherwise, Leigh must surely have known that the woman down the street was dating one of the world's biggest celebrities.

More kids came after that, and although none of the adults accompanying them were quite as shocked to see Max at the door, I could tell they were still impressed that I had him there with me, acting as though he did this sort of thing every day.

In fact, after the first twenty minutes or so of handing out goodies, I got the feeling that the word had spread quickly, because way more people than I would have expected started coming to the house —so many of them, in fact, that the path to the front door was practically choked with trick-or-treaters and their parents, a seemingly endless parade of little goblins and Elsas from *Frozen* and infants in strollers in adorable baby bat and pumpkin costumes.

And even though we'd made dozens and dozens of caramel apples, we ran out a little after seven, and Max had to run to the kitchen to grab his backup bags of Snickers and Twix, and start handing those out.

"So much for having leftovers," he remarked, after what felt like the hundredth group of trick-or-treaters—and their starry-eyed moms—left the porch.

"No kidding," I said. "I'm not sure how long even these are going to last."

As it turned out, we handed over the last Snickers bar at exactly ten minutes after eight, at which point the only thing we could do was lock the front door, turn off the lights in the living room, and retreat to the kitchen.

Max glanced over at the empty cookie sheets I had stacked on the kitchen counters, and let out a suspiciously forlorn sigh. "I didn't even get to have a caramel apple," he said mournfully.

"Fear not, my friend," I replied with a grin. "I thought ahead."

As he watched, I went over to the refrigerator and extracted a box from the back, explaining, "I put a couple of these aside so we could have a more adult Halloween treat."

Inside the box was a pair of eclairs I'd taken from the bakery case at my shop earlier that day. Immediately, Max's eyes lit up.

"I like the way you think."

That was why we ended our Halloween evening sitting at the kitchen table, eating eclairs and drinking very small glasses of cream sherry to go along with our dessert. There was something almost illicit about the way we were hiding back there, especially since the doorbell rang several times during our treat, even though the absolute darkness at the front of the house should have been signal enough that we were no longer handing out candy.

Once he was done with his eclair, Max pushed away his plate and gave a contented sigh. "That was perfect."

"I'm glad you liked it," I replied. Yes, we'd eaten sandwiches in between doling out caramel apples, but they weren't nearly as festive as eclairs and cream sherry. "And now I know I'm going to have to make double the apples for Halloween from now on. I had no idea you'd be such an attraction. I mean, I figured all the local soccer moms would be jaded by your presence by now."

Max shrugged and drank the last of his cream sherry from the little cordial glass I'd given him a while earlier. "I guess not. Maybe it was a little more thrilling to see me face to face instead of just passing me in the toilet paper aisle at Walmart."

About all I could do in response to that comment was shake my head. True, Max actually did a lot of his own shopping, although I knew that Lou and Al also ran errands for him when he was busy or simply didn't feel like driving into town. However, familiarity obviously hadn't bred contempt, or I wouldn't have had such a Halloween rush at the house, thanks to my famous partner-in-crime.

He got up from the table then, and extended a hand. With a smile, he said, "It's still pretty early."

That it was, not even nine o'clock. Plenty of time to have a little dessert following dessert.

"Yes, it is," I agreed, and got up as well so I could place my hand in his. "Time for our own treat, I think."

After all, I couldn't think of a better way to end the evening.

CHAPTER 3

Flying Objects

B ecause I had to be at work early, Max didn't stay the night, but left a little before ten. That was still enough past my bedtime that I was feeling kind of groggy the next morning, although a cup of coffee consumed before I started mixing up the day's muffin batter made me feel a bit better.

Tilly, the talking cat who inhabited the stockroom at the back of the shop, seemed to have survived the night just fine, and was asleep in her bed in a corner of the space when I came in. I'd told her she really needed to come home with me, since Halloween could be dangerous for black cats, but she'd steadfastly refused.

"I've been on my own for years, you know," she'd told me.

I definitely did know, since Tilly repeated that

fact to me pretty much any time I tried to have her stay at the house. Because it was only the truth that she'd lived on the street for years, I knew trying to persuade her otherwise really wasn't worth the effort.

Anyway, she must have had quite a night of it, because she slept right through me coming in and making that first batch of coffee, and only cracked an eyelid when Deanne arrived a little before six.

She was practically grinning. The reason for her amusement became apparent when she remarked, "So, I heard you and Max were the toast of the town last night."

"Yeah, word got around, I guess," I replied. "Thank God Max brought backup candy, or we would have been cowering in the back of the house by seven o'clock."

"That was smart of him," Deanne said as she tied on her apron. "Do you think he guessed you were going to be invaded?"

Good question. I doubted it had been anything premeditated, but I had to admit that Max busted out with some odd prescience from time to time. It wasn't magic, though, but a pretty solid under-standing of human behavior.

"Possibly," I said. "Or maybe he just wanted to play it safe. Either way, it really saved my butt. I made seven dozen caramel apples, but they were gone in an hour."

Deanne's blue eyes widened. "No wonder it was practically a ghost town in our neighborhood. Mike and I wondered what happened, because we've lived there long enough to have a decent idea of how much candy to buy. We hardly gave out any of it, so now we're swimming in the stuff."

There were probably worse things than having too much leftover Halloween candy. I started to say as much, but then Deanne added,

"But Mike took all the leftovers to work with him this morning, except for one bag of Kit Kats. I told him he could leave those."

Even back in high school, Kit Kats had been her favorite kind of candy. Most of the time, she avoided commercial sweets, since she could get much better stuff from me, things that weren't loaded with preservatives and a bunch of chemicals you couldn't pronounce, but she was willing to ignore those concerns when it came to her beloved chocolate-covered wafers.

"That's good," I said. Mike worked for the city, in the department that acted as a liaison with the numerous film and TV production companies that shot their movies and shows in our town, so I guessed he would have plenty of takers for all the leftover candy.

After that exchange, though, it was time to get back to work—me to my muffins and croissants and pastries, and Deanne to head out to the front of the shop to make sure everything would be ready for us to open at seven o'clock. I guessed that the morning would probably be quiet, with many people nursing their sugar hangovers from the day before and not much in the mood to have a pumpkin chocolate-chunk muffin, or whatever.

That was why I was conservative in how much I made that day, figuring I could always throw in an emergency batch of muffins in the late morning if it looked like we wouldn't have enough to last until closing time. Sure enough, business was pretty slow, which was fine by me. Even though I hadn't spent the night before bingeing on Three Musketeers or Reese's peanut butter cups, I still felt kind of sluggish and was just fine with taking things easy.

However, the slow pace of the morning was interrupted by the arrival of Carrie Thomas a little before noon, looking more wild-eyed than I'd ever seen her. "It was destroyed!" she announced, and Deanne and I exchanged a puzzled glance.

"What was destroyed?" I asked.

Carrie pulled in a breath. Her forehead was shiny, as though she'd been perspiring, and she exuded such a sense of anxiety that I could practically feel it pouring off her.

"The Marigold Mural!" she said.

I blinked. Although I hadn't been there to watch every bit of its construction—mostly because Plaza Park was far enough down the street that you couldn't see it from my shop unless you stepped out onto the sidewalk in front—I knew the mural had been quite the undertaking, big pieces of plywood mounted on metal poles that had been driven into the park's grass, with metal connectors and latches holding the pieces of wood together. In all, it was about six feet high and twelve feet long, and definitely not the kind of thing you'd expect to hear had been destroyed.

Especially because Halloween night had been calm and slightly warmer than usual. There had been none of the fierce winds that often rocked northern New Mexico, no torrential rains or any other unusual weather conditions that might have caused some kind of havoc.

"Destroyed how?" Deanne asked.

Carrie pressed her lips together. It looked as though she'd started out her morning wearing some kind of sheer pink gloss, but most of it appeared to have disappeared already. "The poles were torn out of the ground, and the plywood pieces were ripped apart from each other and then broken into pieces. Like I said, it was destroyed."

"I'm so sorry," I said. "I know the decorating committee worked really hard to put it up. Do you need some volunteers to help set up a new one?"

Because even though I wasn't exactly a civil engineer or anything, I figured I could probably provide some assistance. And I knew Max would be happy to pitch in as well—and most likely volunteer Lou and Al to help out, too.

"There's no point in putting it back up," Carrie said flatly, and Deanne sent her a curious look.

"Why not? Do you think the vandals will tear it down again?"

"It wasn't vandals," Carrie replied, still in that flat tone. "It was something much worse."

The edge to her voice made a little shiver make its way down my spine. "What do you mean?"

In response, she pulled an iPhone out of her purse. "We set up security cameras," she said. "We were worried that kids might try to spray-paint on it before we opened the mural for people to leave their messages later today. And we also had a temporary fence around the space. But this happened last night."

She navigated to the media player app, then opened a video. It showed a grainy black and white scene, obviously filmed by the security cameras the Day of the Dead committee had set up near the mural. Sure enough, there it was, a big white expanse faintly blurred by the fence meant to protect it from any of Las Vegas's would-be Banksys.

But then....

First, something seemed to grab hold of the

temporary fence, throwing it aside like it was a big Slinky. After that, the same invisible force went after the mural itself, yanking it off the poles that provided its infrastructure, then tearing the sizeable pieces of plywood away from each other before breaking them into bits.

With this wholesale destruction now complete, the scene went silent and still again.

I looked up from the phone, knowing my eyes were probably as wide as Deanne's. And, even though I couldn't see myself, I had to guess I was also just as white-faced as she was.

"What the hell was that?" she breathed.

However, Carrie Thomas wasn't looking at my best friend. No, she was staring straight at me.

"It had to be a ghost," she said. "And that's why I came here."

Oh, no....

Before I could utter any kind of protest, however, Carrie added, "I need you to talk to it, Skye."

———

"That wasn't a ghost," I said flatly. "That was some kind of berserk poltergeist."

"Still," she insisted. "You're a sort of ghost-whisperer, right? That means you're the only person in Las Vegas who can even communicate with something like that."

My gaze shifted toward Deanne, who was looking just about as dubious as I felt. Okay, I'd helped Ana Moreno—a little ghost girl who'd died in a boiler explosion in the basement of the Plaza Hotel a century ago—move on from the trap of her terrible memories, but still, that didn't mean I was remotely qualified to handle anything like this.

"I don't know—" I began, but Carrie, who'd clearly expected me to offer some kind of protest, wouldn't let me finish.

"Who else can help us?" she cut in. "If we build another mural—which I'm not even sure we have time for—what's to stop this thing from tearing that one down, too?"

Good question. I definitely didn't have an answer for it, mostly because I had absolutely no idea what we were dealing with here.

"Maybe this was a one-off kind of thing," Deanne suggested, although her dubious tone told me she didn't really believe what she was saying.

"And maybe it isn't," Carrie replied. "We can't take that kind of risk, not with the Day of the Dead celebration happening in five days. What if this thing—whatever it is—goes on a rampage with all those families at the park?"

That was a scene I really didn't want to imagine. And while I definitely didn't like the idea of trying to commune with something capable of that kind of destruction, I told myself at least this time I wouldn't have to descend into a dark, creepy basement to do it.

I pulled in a breath and said, "Okay...I'll see what I can do."

Obviously, I had to wait until work was over and the shop safely locked up before I ventured over to Plaza Park. Deanne had offered to come with me, but because I knew spirits could be skittish things, I'd told her it was better that I went alone. For that same reason, I hadn't called Max to request moral support.

After all, how much could go wrong in a public park in broad daylight?

My steps were hesitant as I made my way over to the park at about a quarter to four. The sun was beginning to lower in the sky, but there was plenty of time before it set behind the Sangre de Cristo mountains to the west, and more time still before dusk. A week from now, we'd be back on Standard Time, but for the moment, I was going to take advantage of that extra hour of daylight.

A crew had obviously come along to clean up the mess the entity...ghost, spirit, poltergeist, whatever...had left behind, because the broken boards and torn-up fence were gone. Something gleamed in the frost-yellowed grass, and I bent down to pick it up.

A piece of metal, torn like it was tissue paper or something. I guessed it must have been one of the latches that had held the big pieces of plywood together, but if I hadn't known where it had come from, I would never have recognized it.

Whatever had done this, it must have been very, very angry.

And *very* strong.

Another one of those unwelcome shivers traced its way down my back, and I told myself this was going to be okay. True, I was alone in this section of the park—it looked as though the people out walking their dogs or sitting on the benches had somehow guessed this was not the place to be—but they were still close enough that they'd definitely hear me if I called for help.

Or at least, I hoped they were.

I put my hands on my hips and looked all around me, but on the surface, everything appeared completely normal—the big cottonwoods with their leaves now displaying their full autumn gold, the concrete path that wound its way through grass beginning to get patchy at the tail end of fall. Although I'd never bothered to count all those walks, I knew I must have gone through this section of the park hundreds of times in my life, and I'd never noticed anything odd or off about it. The mural had been erected on the south side of the park, opposite my side of the street, but I still went this way a lot because it was the most direct route to get to the police station, which often got any muffins or other pastries that might be left over at the end of my workday.

Still, something felt off right now, although I couldn't say for sure whether that was because there really was some kind of entity lurking nearby, or whether my imagination was playing tricks on me.

Then again, *something* had torn up the mural... and it sure hadn't been a couple of kids with vandalism on their minds.

At the very edge of my vision, something seemed to flicker. I turned, and caught the faintest glimpse of a shape that might have been human.

Once.

It was gone before I could even try to focus on it, though. Maybe it had realized I'd detected its presence—or maybe it was simply that someone had finally come along this stretch of walkway, a woman with a golden retriever practically dragging her down the path. She sent me an apologetic smile as she went past, and I smiled in return. I didn't recognize her, which wasn't too strange. Yes, I'd lived in Las Vegas my entire life, and a good chunk of the population seemed to come in and out of my shop on a regular basis, but I still couldn't pretend to know everyone who lived here.

After the woman and her golden retriever had reached the sidewalk and crossed the street, I turned back to the space between the two big cottonwood trees, hoping maybe I'd catch another flicker of that whatever-it-was now I was alone again.

But even though I waited a good five minutes, I could tell it didn't plan on returning right now. Part of me wanted to take that as a sign, and that I could tell Carrie Thomas that I'd done my best but hadn't been able to detect anything.

Unfortunately, I knew that would be a major cop-out. And although I supposed I could try to convince myself this wasn't my problem, that I wasn't the one organizing the Day of the Dead festival, that seemed like a cowardly thing to do. Poor little Las Vegas had had so many deaths and scandals over the past year, and I really didn't want our brand-new event to be dead on arrival before it had a chance of becoming a tradition. People traveled from as far away as Albuquerque and Red River to come to our harvest festival, and I knew Carrie—and the mayor—hoped that the Día de los Muertos celebration would become another reason for people to visit our town.

And, as Deanne had pointed out on more than

one occasion, anything that brought people to Las Vegas meant more business for Levitation Latte.

No, if I wanted to get to the bottom of this, I knew I'd have to do something I really wasn't looking forward to.

I'd have to come back to Plaza Park after dark.

CHAPTER 4

Back to the Future

I'd had plans to go over to Max's that night, plans I knew I'd have to cancel. True, I supposed I could have had dinner with him and headed to the park afterward, but that didn't seem like a very good idea. For one thing, I needed to be clear-headed when I tried to approach the entity in the park, something that seemed like it would be hard to do after a glass of wine. And okay, I could have skipped the alcohol for one night, but then he'd probably ask why.

Of course, he asked anyway, when I called him after I got home and told him something had come up.

"'Something'?" he repeated. "Like what?"

I hesitated. Max wasn't as tuned in to the local gossip as a lot of other people, mostly because he lived away from town and didn't have any neighbors to chat with, and partly because, besides Deanne and Mike and me, he didn't mingle as much as I'd thought he might. Back in high school, he'd been the popular guy, a star quarterback who also had the lead role in every play, and sometimes it seemed as though he was friends with practically everyone at our school.

But after his high school sweetheart wanted to get back with him and her jealous husband had tried to frame him for murder, Max had pulled back a little. Not that he wasn't friendly...but I also noticed that he hadn't made any overtures to get together with the group of guys who'd been his squad back in the day.

I'd asked him about it not too long ago, and he'd looked almost uncomfortable. "We don't have much in common anymore," he told me, which was easy enough to believe. "I mean, I'll invite them to my parties because I want people to have a good time, but that's about it for socializing. Also, a couple of the guys tried to hit me up for money, and that left a real bitter taste in my mouth. I don't mind pitching in when I see a need, but I also don't like knowing that some people view me as an ATM or something just because we used to be friends."

That was the first time he'd said anything about the current situation with his former buddies, and I had to admit it was pretty uncomfortable, especially when you considered how generous Max had been after moving to town, whether it was setting up a trust for Raylene's kids so they'd be able to stay in their house and go to college or whatever they wanted, despite their father being in prison for at least the next twenty-five years, or paying to finish all the projects the *Fix My Town* team had started and then abruptly shut down after one of their producers murdered the show's executive producer. Max had never come out and said exactly who had been asking for money, and I hadn't probed further, knowing the issue was a sensitive one for him.

Anyway, I guessed he probably hadn't heard about how the mural had been destroyed. It would have been nice to keep him blissfully oblivious and make up some kind of white lie or another for why I was canceling our dinner date, but I'd vowed always to tell him the truth, no matter what.

So, I launched into a quick explanation of what had gone down at Plaza Park, and described as best I could the video Carrie Thomas had shown Deanne and me.

"It's really obvious something supernatural is going on," I concluded. "But trying to figure it out in daylight didn't turn out so well. That's why I need to go back after dark."

"I'm coming with you," Max said at once, a response I'd expected...and hoped I could deflect without too much arguing.

"I don't think that's a good idea," I countered. "I get the feeling this entity—whatever it is— doesn't like people very much. It'll be better if I'm by myself."

A pause. I couldn't see Max's face, but I had a feeling he was frowning. "You said you saw a video of this thing tearing apart big chunks of plywood that had been bolted together. Do you really think it's smart to be there without backup?"

On the surface, probably not. On the other hand, people had been coming and going in that section of the park for years without getting decked by a garbage can or something, so I didn't think I was taking too big a risk.

I hoped.

No, the entity had vented its ire on the mural in particular, for whatever reason. I had to hope I'd be able to communicate with it and figure out exactly why the Day of the Dead festival had gotten under its skin...so to speak.

"Max, I'm pretty sure it won't show up if you're there," I said.

"How do you know that?"

"Call it a gut feeling," I replied, which was only the truth. "I'm just going on instinct here."

Another of those pauses. Then he let out a breath and said, "I don't want anything to happen to you."

"I don't want anything to happen to me,

either," I responded. "But I think it's going to be okay. Also, if anything turns weird, I can run over to the police station. You know it's only a few minutes away."

"I suppose," Max said, now sounding almost grudging. However, because he hadn't bothered to protest that extremely obvious fact, I got the feeling he knew he was running out of arguments.

"It'll be fine," I assured him again. "I'm going to eat something here, then go over to the park as soon as it's full dark, like a little after seven-thirty. I doubt it's going to take me very long, so I'll call you as soon as I get home."

"You'd better," he said. "And if I don't hear from you by eight at the very latest, then I'm going over there—and I'm bringing police backup."

Since I had no idea how long a conversation with this spirit might take, that felt as if it might be cutting things a little close. However, I didn't argue. There was every chance that I'd get to the park and still not see a damn thing, which meant I'd be back home way before Max's eight o'clock cut-off time.

"It's a deal," I said. "Honestly, I don't know if I'm going to encounter anything at all."

"Here's hoping you don't," he replied. "I know you're trying to help, but...."

"I know," I said. I couldn't really be angry with him for thinking maybe this was somebody else's problem and I shouldn't be putting my safety on the line, not when similar thoughts had crossed through my mind not so long ago. "And I won't take any chances, I promise."

That reassurance seemed to be enough to mollify him, because he said, "Okay. Just...be careful. I don't know what I'd do if I lost you."

Those words were utterly sincere, and enough to send a pang of doubt through me. Maybe this wasn't worth the risk.

But then I told myself I'd already promised Carrie I would help. Besides, I'd had other encounters with ghosts, and while they'd been creepy and ultimately sad, I'd escaped those meetings unscathed. Nothing here should be any different.

Well, except the way this particular ghost rips up sheets of plywood like it's toilet paper, I thought.

I shivered, and was glad Max wasn't here to see my obvious worry. Doing my best to sound confident, I replied, "You're not going to lose me, Max. It's going to be fine...and we'll have something to talk about when you come over for lasagna tomorrow night."

"Lasagna?" he repeated, a hopeful note in his voice. "That would be awesome. But I'm going to want a report way sooner than that. I'm calling you at eight, remember?"

Right. "True," I said, "but I'm still making you lasagna."

"And those garlic knots?"

"Absolutely," I replied, even as I reflected it was good that Max had an amazing metabolism...and the time to work out in his home gym for at least an hour every day. As far as I'd been able to tell, he'd never met a carb he didn't like.

Because I also had the enviable ability to eat pretty much whatever I wanted without having to worry about it, we had some pretty fun dinners together.

"Okay," he said. "I'll talk to you at eight. Be careful, Skye."

"I will," I said, and added, "Love you."

"Love you, too."

That was how we ended all our phone calls. Maybe those words should have become stale with repetition, but not so far. I still thrilled down to my toes every time I heard Max utter those three small but so important words.

I set down the phone and glanced out the window at the backyard. Some of the trees were already bare, giving me a good look at the sky, which had begun to warm as the sun set behind the mountains.

In a little less than two hours, I had a date with a ghost.

At that hour of the evening, no one was loitering in Plaza Park. In the summer, when the days were warm and dusk lingered until almost nine, you'd usually see a couple of people hanging out, either walking their dogs or simply sitting on the park benches and enjoying the mild night air. Tonight, though, despite our above-average temperatures lately, it wasn't comfortable enough to spend much time here unless you were cutting across the park to get to one of the businesses on the other side.

But they were all closed, except for the ice cream shop, which always stayed stubbornly open until eight no matter how cold it was outside. It didn't look as though they had many takers this evening, however; I could tell that their lights were on, but I didn't see anyone coming and going from the place.

Still, just knowing the ice cream shop's door was open and someone was working inside made me feel a little better. That meant they'd hear me if I screamed.

Probably.

Because I'd caught that single glimpse of the entity under one of the two cottonwoods that stood next to the open area where the mural had been erected, I went over there now. I'd put on a puffer jacket but hadn't zipped it up, although I had my fingers jammed in the pockets to keep my hands warm.

Or maybe it wasn't the barely fifty-degree temperatures outside that had made me chilled all over, but the realization that something was here, watching me.

I couldn't even say how I knew that, only that the cool evening air seemed to grow utterly still, as if the world was holding its breath, waiting to see what would happen next.

"Are you there?" I asked, knowing how tentative those words sounded. I could have told myself I was only self-conscious about standing in that spot under the cottonwood and speaking out loud to the empty space, but I knew better. While it was necessary for me to reach out to the ghost, that didn't mean I had to like it.

No reply, only that same unnatural stillness. At this time of night, the leaves on the trees were almost always a-flutter, because northern New Mexico was a place of strong breezes, whether they were the cold north winds of winter or the warm, unruly ones that drove monsoon storms out of the Gulf of Mexico.

But I could somehow sense the spirit's presence, feel it like a weight against my skin. It hadn't been like this when I'd encountered Ana Moreno's ghost in the basement of the Plaza Hotel. Yes, at first I'd been frightened because I hadn't known who—or what—was causing that chill down my spine, but still, I'd only felt cold, not like something was pushing against me, making it hard to breathe.

In fact, it almost felt like hands around my throat, squeezing.

I gasped, and forced in a breath of chilly night air. "Stop it!"

At once, the pressure eased. Again, I caught that flicker at the corner of my eyes, only this time it didn't disappear.

No, it grew clearer, more solid. Now I could see it really was a human shape, resolving into the form of a girl who looked like she was probably fifteen or sixteen, with long, straight pale hair, a heart-shaped face, and eyes whose color I couldn't quite make out, but which I guessed had probably been blue when she was alive.

And, after taking a quick glance at her clothing, which consisted of a slouchy sweater slipping off one shoulder, a short polka-dot skirt, and a pair of leg warmers, I had to believe she must have died in the 1980s. Or at least, I knew I'd never seen anyone dress like that outside movies or TV shows that had been filmed around that time. Okay, if she'd been a true child of the eighties, she should have had hair that was permed and teased to the point of torture, but still, her clothes were a dead giveaway as to the decade when she'd left this mortal coil.

Because she appeared to me in gray-scale, I

couldn't really tell what color the getup had been in real life, but I thought it had probably been hot pink and screaming lime green, or something equally obnoxious.

"You can see me," she said. Her voice was light and pretty, almost breathy.

I nodded. "That's kind of a thing I can do," I replied. "Talk to ghosts, I mean."

At once, her bow-shaped mouth formed into a pout. "Don't say that word."

"'Ghost'?" I repeated, and her lips pressed even more tightly together.

"Yeah, that one," she said. "I don't want to think about it."

So, a ghost who wasn't too happy with her incorporeal state. I supposed I couldn't really blame her. If nothing else, it had to have been kind of boring to be stuck hanging around a park for thirty-plus years. Also, something awful had to have happened to her for her to be moored here. Although spirits didn't always haunt the places where they died, my personal experience told me that if someone died in a tragic or violent way, then there was a much greater chance that they'd remain rooted to the place where they'd met their demise.

"Okay," I said, telling myself to make sure I chose my words carefully, "let's just say I've talked to other people like you."

She crossed her arms. "There's no one else here

'like me.' The other ghosts in this town are a bunch of old fuddy-duddies."

There was a word I hadn't heard in a while. But then, if the girl standing in front of me now hadn't died before she really even started living, she would have been in her fifties by now, someone of my mother's generation, even though she looked almost half my age.

However, it wasn't her vocabulary that startled me now. "You can talk to the other ghosts?" I demanded.

A lift of the shoulder that was revealed by her slouchy shaker-knit sweater. "Some of them." She paused, and I could have sworn she shuddered a bit. "Others are gross, and I stay far away from those ones. Like that creepy guy at the hotel."

She tilted her head toward the Plaza, now only a dim bulk on the other side of the park, with a few yellow rectangles showing the rooms that were currently occupied.

Her remark made me want to shudder as well. Even though Ana and Miguel Moreno had moved on to the next plane, the spirit of their terrible grandfather, the man who'd abused them and perished along with his grandchildren when the boiler in the hotel's basement blew, remained behind, destined to suffer eternally for the crimes he'd committed.

As far as I was concerned, that wasn't enough

punishment for what he'd done, but at least it was a start.

"Just one creepy guy?" I asked, thinking of the ghost of Byron T. Wells, who'd been one of the Plaza Hotel's early owners and who now haunted the third floor of the building, where his office had once been located. I'd never experienced any of this personally—all I'd felt was a cold spot when I'd walked past that room—but I'd heard through the grapevine that Byron T's ghost could get a little handsy around attractive women.

The spirit in front of me nodded. "Yeah. There's the ghost of the guy who owned the hotel or something, but he's more protective of me than anything."

Well, that was something. I supposed it was good to know that Mr. Wells might have been a lech, but only with women who were of age.

"What's your name?" I asked next, glad that this particular ghost spoke perfect English. Communicating with Ana Moreno had been laborious, mostly because her English wasn't very good and the remnants of my high school Spanish had been even worse.

The teenage ghost flipped her long, pale hair. Because it probably had been very light even when she was alive, her current black-and-white appearance hadn't changed its color very much.

"Mandy," she said. "Mandy Carson."

The name wasn't familiar to me. But then, why would it be? This girl had been dead much longer than I'd been alive, and any scandal connected to her murder would have died down—no pun intended—way before I was born.

However, there were still a couple of people named Carson who lived in Las Vegas. Her relatives? Not her parents; Jackie Carson was in her late forties, which meant she was a little younger than the apparition I faced would have been if she'd still been alive. And there was Barbara Carson, who was definitely in her early eighties but still drove around Las Vegas in a meticulously maintained Lincoln that had to be at least twenty years old.

Was she Mandy's mother?

I couldn't remember off-hand if either Jackie or Barbara had ever mentioned a family member named Mandy who'd been murdered in Plaza Park back in the 1980s. Then again, it wasn't the sort of topic that came up when you were ordering a latte.

"Can you tell me what happened to you?" I said.

At once, Mandy's mouth formed into another of those pouts. She definitely wasn't the kind of girl I would have hung out with—everything about her, despite those crazy '80s clothes, practically screamed popular girl, maybe a cheerleader, while I'd been a skinny, dark late bloomer—but I couldn't deny that she'd been very pretty. Even her current monotone appearance couldn't hide the long blonde hair or the regular features and full mouth.

"I don't know what happened," she replied. "I mean, someone strangled me, but I couldn't see who it was."

I thought of the choking sensation I'd first experienced when I stepped into this small open space between the two cottonwoods, how it felt like someone had wrapped their hands around my throat. Although I didn't know how such a thing even worked, I had to believe that must have been Mandy exerting some sort of influence on the physical world around her, performing some sort of grisly re-enactment of the way she'd died as a knee-jerk reaction to someone invading her space.

Poor kid.

"Why tear down the mural?" I said then. "I mean, there've been plenty of events held in this park since—" I broke off there, realizing right before the words left my lips that it probably wouldn't be very tactful to come right out and say that she'd been murdered in this spot. "Anyway," I went on hastily, "it's not like there haven't been plenty of people coming and going since then."

The ghost girl's pale eyes blazed with sudden anger. "Yeah, I know," she snapped. "Because I've been here for probably every single one of those stupid events. It made me mad that the people in this town wouldn't stay away from this spot, but I just figured it was because they didn't know what had happened to me. But then they started setting up for that Day of the Dead thingy, and it just pissed me off. It's all about honoring the dead, but did anyone honor me? No," she continued, before I could even begin to open my mouth. "There's not even a stupid plaque here to mark the place where I died, and the person who killed me is still out there somewhere. So screw your stupid Day of the Dead festival!"

After spitting out that comment, Mandy abruptly disappeared. I blinked and looked around, but there was no sign of her...and I guessed she had no plans to return tonight, not even if I stood here and tried to call out to her again.

I released a sigh, then began making my way across the park, mind churning.

Mandy wanted to be remembered and was angry that her killer still walked free. He or she had to be in their fifties by now, maybe more. Who was to say they were even in Las Vegas? If I'd committed that kind of heinous wrongdoing and gotten away with it, I would have made sure to go far, far away from the scene of the crime.

But despite all that, I knew what I had to do if the Day of the Dead festival was going to happen at all.

To appease Mandy's ghost, I'd have to figure

out who murdered her, and make sure she was remembered. How the hell I was supposed to solve a murder that was decades old, I had absolutely no idea.

If I didn't, though...if I failed...that festival definitely wasn't happening.

CHAPTER 5

Dirty Deeds

As overwhelmed as I was feeling about the whole situation, though, I didn't forget about calling Max to let him know I was okay. He answered before his phone even had a chance to ring twice, and said, "Are you all right?"

"I'm fine," I replied tiredly. Something about that encounter with Mandy's ghost had seemed to drain me somehow, although I told myself that was only because I'd suddenly found myself confronted by what appeared to be an insurmountable task. "There's definitely a ghost in that spot in the park. Her name was Mandy Carson. Have you ever heard of her? It looks like she died back in the '80s sometime, judging by her clothes."

"No, I haven't," Max responded at once, something I'd been expecting. He was only a year older than I, so it wasn't as though he'd have any more access to decades'-old crime information than I would. "Did she tell you what happened to her?"

"Sounds like she was strangled," I said. "And she's angry that no one remembers her, and that's why she's messing up the Day of the Dead festival. I'm pretty sure unless I get this figured out and get her some justice, she's not going to let the festival happen."

Max let out a breath. "That sucks."

"Tell me about it." More than anything, I wished he was here with me now, rather than a couple of miles away at his ranch on the east end of town. Just feeling his arms around me would have made me feel a lot better about the situation.

But I'd told him I was going to handle this problem on my own, and that meant I needed to be an adult about the whole thing.

"So...what's next?" he asked.

Luckily, I'd already been pondering that conundrum on my drive home. "I'm going to try doing some research online right now," I replied. "Maybe someone put Mandy's case on a true crime website or something. Problem is, the crime happened so many years ago, I'm not sure how much I'm going to find."

"Well, we can always go to the historical society tomorrow after you're off work," Max suggested. "We found some good stuff there when we were trying to find out what happened with the hotel's boiler explosion."

True, we had. Not all the details, obviously—the locals had done their best to sweep the children's deaths in the explosion under the rug—but even so, the old newspapers we'd found there had provided a few useful clues. All that had happened way back in the 1920s, while we'd be trying to find information about a crime that had occurred in the '80s. I had to hope there'd be a lot more material available about something so comparatively recent.

"Sounds like a plan," I replied. "Meet me at the shop at a quarter to four?"

"It's a date," he said. "Then maybe we can come back here for dinner."

Because I wanted to see him, I didn't protest that it was a weeknight and that I had to get up early the next day. Maybe we could brainstorm, maybe figure out something from whatever clues we might have located.

I had to hope so. It was already Wednesday, and that meant I had only a few days to solve a crime that had been unsolved for decades. If I didn't...

...well, I wouldn't worry about that right now.

Right now, I had some research to do.

To my surprise, I actually located a mention of Mandy Carson's murder, on a website put together by someone who'd decided to keep a database of unsolved murders in New Mexico. There wasn't much information, but at least now I knew that her full name was Mandy Elizabeth Carson, and that she'd been sixteen years old when she died on a cool October night in 1985. The local police investigated, of course, but no evidence pointing to the crime was ever found, and it became a cold case about five years later.

It wasn't much, but a little was better than nothing. I wrote what I knew in a text file on my laptop, figuring that at least knowing the date would help Dorothy Innes, the woman who ran the historical society, find any relevant newspaper clippings regarding Mandy Carson's murder.

For now, though, it was time to go to sleep.

Sometimes I had true dreams about the various murder investigations I got embroiled in, but tonight wasn't that night. I had a few vague, blurry dreams that seemed to involve the horses on Max's ranch turning into unicorns and the two of us riding through meadows that looked vaguely like the poppy fields from *The Wizard of Oz,* but none of that seemed too relevant to the problem at hand.

The next morning at work, I filled Deanne in on what had happened the night before, then asked her if she'd ever heard anything about Mandy Carson's murder.

"No," she said at once. "But maybe one of my mom's friends would know. I mean, we moved to Las Vegas when I was a kid, so it's not like she went to school here, but most of her friends are natives."

Just as I was. People came and went from Las Vegas, of course, leaving to seek better prospects in larger towns, but a good number of them stayed put or came back after deciding they really didn't want to live anywhere else. I had to believe that at least a couple of Libby Gardner's—Deanne's mom —friends had gone to high school with Mandy Carson, and therefore would know a heck of a lot more about her than I could ever find in an old newspaper clipping.

"Can you check?" I asked. "I already have a date with Max to go to the historical society after work today, but maybe we could talk to one of your mom's friends afterward."

"Will do," Deanne said, her face now glowing with excitement. I knew she'd been a little bummed about missing out on my previous investigation— not to mention also not being here for the momentous occasion of Max and I finally declaring our love for one another—so I could tell she was happy to be of assistance now.

In fact, she hurried into the back so she could get her phone out of her purse in the cubby where she usually kept it, presumably to shoot off a quick text to her mother. Because we hadn't even opened yet—it was about a quarter to seven—she probably figured it was okay to leave me alone for a few minutes.

And it was. I restocked the napkin containers and got a pot of decaf going, and by the time I was done, she'd returned to the front of the shop, expression triumphant.

"My mom's best friend Evelyn totally went to school with Mandy," Deanne informed me.

"I hope your mother wasn't bugging Evelyn this early in the morning," I commented. It was one thing for Deanne to reach out to her own mother at this ungodly hour, since I assumed she knew whether or not it was okay, but I really didn't want to be responsible for Libby Gardner waking up her best friend before seven o'clock.

"She didn't have to," Deanne replied, looking unperturbed. "She said she remembered how Evelyn told her about how her friend Mandy had been killed their junior year of high school, and how much it shook everyone up. I guess none of the girls went anywhere alone for like a year after that or something."

Which wasn't too surprising. If one of my classmates had been killed in such a heinous way and the murderer had never been caught, I would have made sure to have a buddy with me at all times...preferably the linebacker from my high school's football team.

Unless the linebacker was the one responsible.

"Sounds like I need to talk to Evelyn," I said. "Do you have her number? I'll try to call her later and see if maybe she can meet with me and Max late this afternoon."

"Oh, I'm sure she'll talk to you," Deanne replied, blue eyes now dancing with amusement. "She's got a huge crush on Max."

I hadn't really thought about how having Max as my investigative assistant might open a few doors, but now I realized that, besides being the most amazing man I'd ever met, his star power could help me gain access to people who might otherwise have had any reason to talk to me.

"Convenient," I said, matching my best friend's grin with one of my own.

Deanne gave me Evelyn's number, and I stored her contact information on my phone, which I always carried with me in my apron pocket. Obviously, I'd have to wait for a more socially acceptable hour to call and confirm that she was willing to give us an interview, but I was still glad I had a backup plan set in place.

As it turned out, Evelyn was more than thrilled to talk to Max and me, and we set up a meeting for five-thirty at her house, when she'd be home from work. That meshed perfectly with my previous plans, because that way, Max and I would have plenty of time to go to the historical society and do some sleuthing there before we had to head over to Evelyn's place, which was about ten minutes away, at one of the "ranchettes" on the northwest side of town.

Things got busy enough at the coffee shop after our telephone exchange that I didn't have much of a chance to do more than text Max to let him know about going to Evelyn's house.

Hope that doesn't upset your dinner plans too much.

No, it's fine. I'll just push dinner to seven instead of six-thirty. Or do you think we'll need more time than that?

I don't think so. It sounded like Evelyn didn't have a lot of time before she had to start making dinner for her family.

Okay. Dinner at seven, then.

I sent him a thumbs-up, and that seemed to take care of things.

Of course, I wasn't entirely thrilled to see Carrie Thomas show up at three, at the same time a group of high school kids came in to clear out my leftover muffins and get a bunch of lattes and chai tea. Luckily, Deanne came to my rescue, handling their orders so I could go over and talk to the mayor's assistant.

"Anything new?" she said. Today she looked

even more nervous than she had the last time she stopped in, and I couldn't say I blamed her. With the Day of the Dead festival slated to begin two days from now, I didn't have much time to get all this straightened out.

"A few developments," I replied, although I'd already told myself I shouldn't give her too many details this early on. Maybe her knowing the ghost haunting the park was Mandy Carson's spirit wouldn't change anything, but I also couldn't rule out her getting so stressed about the entire situation that she might call in Father Salvador, the priest at the local Catholic church, to sprinkle some holy water around the place in an attempt to banish the specter.

Somehow, I knew that would be disastrous. Mandy really didn't seem like the type to respond well to intervention by an authority figure.

"I have a couple of leads," I went on, in response to Carrie's inquiring sandy eyebrows. "I'm going to follow up on both of them right after I'm off work today."

She didn't exactly relax, but something about her stance seemed slightly less tense. "What did you find?"

"I'm not sure yet," I said. "Like I said, they're just leads. I don't want to talk about it too much until I have more to go on."

That answer definitely didn't sit well with her,

because her lips compressed and she said, "We're running out of time."

Tell me something I don't know, I thought. But because I didn't want to get into a confrontation with the mayor's assistant when a bunch of curious sixteen-year-olds was standing just a few yards away, I only shook my head and replied, "I don't want to jinx it. Maybe it's nothing. As soon as I have something more concrete, I'll let you know."

She let out a breath that wasn't quite a huff and looked as though she was going to respond with an angry retort. However, she also seemed to realize this wasn't the best place for an argument—or maybe she figured out that pissing off the town's one and only ghost whisperer wasn't such a great idea—because she only said, "All right. We'll do it your way. But if we can't be in that park by 8 a.m. to set up on Saturday morning, then this thing isn't going to happen."

No pressure.

"I'm doing everything I can," I assured her. "And I've got Max helping me. The festival is going to happen, I promise."

"I certainly hope so," Carrie said. "The mayor is freaking out."

Somehow, I doubted that Alex Donnelly, our current mayor, was even capable of "freaking out." He'd been an accountant before he became deputy mayor and then took over the mayor's position after Tom Gallegos was murdered, and he seemed constitutionally incapable of getting flustered about pretty much anything.

Then again, losing the Day of the Dead festival would mean losing tourists, and that meant lost revenue. That was about the only thing I could think of that might actually upset him, so maybe Carrie hadn't been embellishing the truth as much as I'd thought she had.

"I'll keep you updated," I said, and she seemed to understand I had nothing else to contribute for now, because she released another one of those semi-annoying huffs of a breath before replying,

"I hope you do."

She left, and the group of high school kids who'd been lingering nearby went to take their seats at the pair of purple velvet couches I had set up in a far corner of the store. Seeing this, I tried not to sigh. The last thing I needed was them hanging around past closing.

No, I needed to get out of here right at three-thirty.

To my relief, though, they all finished their drinks and their snacks faster than I'd thought they would, and even paused to drop everything in the trash on their way out. Right as they were leaving, though, one girl paused near me where I was wiping down another table, getting ready for closing.

"You're the chick who talks to ghosts, right?" she asked.

For a second, I thought about telling her she had the wrong person, but then I realized that was silly. It was a small town; everyone knew who I was, and how I'd helped Ana Moreno's ghost to ascend only a few months earlier.

"Well, sometimes I do," I answered, figuring that was slightly better than coming right out and admitting I had a talent no one else I knew seemed to share.

The girl—she looked like she was probably the same age Mandy had been when she was murdered, although I knew Mandy's hair had never been dyed bright blue the way this girl's was—sent a quick glance over at the rest of her group, but since they were talking and laughing and roughhousing a little, they didn't seem to be paying any attention to the way their friend had paused to talk to the coffee shop owner.

"It's kind of a game some of us played in grade school," the girl said in a confiding whisper. "You know, like Bloody Mary in the mirror?"

Since I remembered doing that at the slumber parties I'd attended—always at Deanne's house, since she'd been my one and only real friend—I nodded.

"Well, we did that," the blue-haired girl told

me, her voice dropping even lower. "Except it was with the girl murdered in the park."

About all I could do was blink back at her. This was the first time I'd had any inkling that anyone still remembered what had happened to Mandy Carson. After all, I'd grown up in Las Vegas and spent my whole life here, and I sure as hell hadn't known a single thing about her murder until I went and talked to her in the park last night.

"Did she answer?" I asked, genuinely curious.

The girl shook her bright blue head. "Nope. But after I heard about what happened to that mural thing, and how you were wandering around in the park last night, talking to no one, I remembered that game we used to play."

And here I'd thought I was entirely alone. At least, I definitely hadn't seen anyone nearby while I was having my convo with Mandy, but it seemed that didn't mean much. Who had heard me? One of the workers in the ice cream store across the street?

In the end, it probably didn't matter too much, except I vowed to be even more careful in the future. While I was generally accepted now—Levitation Latte was one of Las Vegas's most popular spots, and having it known that I was Max Sullivan's significant other hadn't hurt, either—I really didn't want everyone to think I was a total crackpot.

"Where did you learn the game?" I asked, and the girl shrugged.

"At a friend's house," she said. "Lake Palmer."

I had no idea who Lake Palmer was, but I knew I'd find out soon enough. It wasn't exactly a common name. "Do you know where Lake found out about it?"

Another lift of the girl's shoulders. She was wearing a Cure T-shirt, probably bought at Hot Topic while visiting Santa Fe or Albuquerque, and was pretty in a thin, intense kind of way. "Maybe one of her cousins or something? I don't think she told us. It was just something to do while we were hanging out."

Hmm. It seemed pretty obvious to me that the girl didn't know exactly where the urban legend had originated, but someone had to have started sharing it. A former classmate of Mandy's, possibly a friend who missed her and thought maybe she could get some kind of message from beyond?

Without a lot more facts in hand, there was no way to know for sure.

But Max and I would be talking to Deanne's mom's friend Evelyn in just a little while, and I could ask her if she'd ever heard about Las Vegas's own particular version of the "Bloody Mary in the mirror" game. Someone clearly had known about it, or they wouldn't have handed it down to the town's younger generation.

"Hey, Allie," one boy in the group of high school kids called out. "You planning to hang around here all day?"

"Gotta go," said the blue-haired girl. "I just thought it was something you'd like to know."

I thanked her, even as she hurried over to join the rest of their friends. A minute later, they were gone, the door banging shut behind them.

"What did she want?" Deanne asked, obviously curious to know why a high school kid like that would need to talk to an old lady like me.

Okay, I'd only turned thirty a few weeks earlier, but it still felt way older than twenty-nine.

"Have you ever heard of a 'Bloody Mary in the mirror' slumber party game, but about Mandy Carson?"

Looking mystified, Deanne shook her head. "No. Is there one?"

"Sounds like it. I just don't know what it means."

Maybe it was nothing. Still, I was very curious to hear what Evelyn would have to say on the subject.

CHAPTER 6

Ever After

"No, I've definitely never heard of anything like that," Evelyn Hodge told Max and me in emphatic tones. "Honestly, I think it's in pretty poor taste."

I had to agree. It was one thing to turn a historical figure into the object of a slumber-party game, but to do the same thing to a girl who'd passed away only a few decades earlier seemed insensitive at best.

The three of us were sitting in Evelyn's living room, which was much more modern than the modest exterior of her ranch-style home might have indicated. It seemed obvious to me that she spent a lot of time watching home decorating shows in her free time, because the pale wood floors, ivory sofas, and gray kitchen cabinets looked as though they'd come right out of a home makeover that might have aired just last week. The only slightly out-of-place item was an old spinet set against one wall. But even though it didn't exactly match the rest of the decor, it had probably been a family heirloom, something she hadn't wanted to get rid of.

We'd come here after our trip to the historical society, which had been pretty much a bust. None of the local papers from that time provided any more information than what we'd already been able to glean, which was why we were now pinning our hopes on Evelyn Hodge.

She was a woman in her early fifties, with hair that had gone gray early. In fact, the color looked so consistent that I wondered whether she'd had a stylist help the gray along, but whether it was natural or not, it definitely complemented her fair skin and blue-gray eyes. Maybe she carried a little extra weight, and yet it looked good on her, making sure she had very few wrinkles or lines yet.

And I could tell she was trying her hardest not to stare at Max, or to pinch herself to make sure she wasn't dreaming, that Max Sullivan really was seated across the glass and steel coffee table from her.

"Mandy Carson was my best friend," she said softly, clear eyes misted with pain even after all these years. "When I heard the news, I couldn't believe it. Everyone loved Mandy."

Those words made me wonder whether Evelyn

was embellishing the truth just a little. I couldn't admit to a huge acquaintance with Mandy, of course, but even our brief exchange had given me the impression that she'd been kind of a brat.

Then again, being trapped in teenage ghost form in a public park for almost forty years was probably enough to put anyone in a bad mood.

"What can you tell us about her?" Max put in, and a little flush rose to Evelyn's cheeks.

Deanne definitely hadn't been exaggerating when she'd told me her mother's best friend had a huge crush on Max Sullivan.

But despite being clearly overwhelmed by such a celebrity's presence in her living room, Evelyn seemed to do her best to focus on his question. "She was very popular," she said. "Head of the cheerleading squad even as a junior, friends with almost everyone. She was a good student, too."

Mandy definitely sounded like a paragon... although I reminded myself that time could smooth away almost anyone's rough edges.

"So, there wasn't anyone you could think of who might have wanted to hurt her?" I asked, and immediately, Evelyn shook her head.

"The police back then asked me the same thing —asked all the girls in our group. But none of us had any idea who might have done such an awful thing."

"No one who was jealous of her?" Max said

next. "Or maybe one of the boys in school who wanted to be with her and couldn't?"

That question seemed to bother Evelyn, because she pressed her lips together and didn't reply for a moment. When she spoke, however, she seemed ready to shoot down that particular idea.

"I'm pretty sure there were lots of boys in our school who had crushes on her," she told us. "But I can't believe any of them would kill her just because he couldn't go out with her. Also, she had a boyfriend on the football team, and because he was kind of a big guy, people knew he would do anything to protect her."

Next to me, Max shifted on the sofa. He didn't say anything, but I could guess what he was thinking.

"Who was he?" I asked. I didn't want to be one to stereotype, but a "big guy" on the football team sounded like exactly the sort of person with the size and strength to choke Mandy Carson to death. "What kind of relationship did he and Mandy have? Do you think there's any way he could have been involved?"

Now Evelyn released a breath, and I noticed how her fingers played with the wide white gold wedding band on her ring finger. "Her boyfriend was Jeff Hodge."

I shot a startled glance over at Max, whose

expression seemed to be equally shocked. "'Hodge'?" he repeated.

Evelyn gave both of us a rueful smile. "Yes, Jeff is my husband. We consoled each other after Mandy's death, and...." The words trailed off, but it was easy enough to put two and two together, and guess that they'd come to realize they had feelings for each other. "Anyway," she went on, her tone brisker now, "Jeff had absolutely nothing to do with it. The police questioned him, obviously, but there wasn't anything to find—he was innocent, of course, and could prove he was at a football game miles away in Estancia the night she was murdered. I'd been planning to go to the game, but my little sister was sick and my parents needed me to stay home and watch her."

So much for that. If Jeff hadn't had a rock-solid alibi to prove he had been nowhere near Plaza Park on the night in question, I might have tried digging a little further into that topic, even if doing so might have upset Evelyn. But since the police had already explored that lead and come to a dead end, I didn't see the point in pursuing it.

Before I could say anything in reply to her comment, Evelyn went on, "The murder was thoroughly investigated. The police interviewed what seemed like almost everyone in this town, but they never found anything. No suspects, nothing. That's why it's been a cold case all these years."

And so far, it didn't seem as though I was going to discover anything that would blow it wide open, either. Part of me wanted to just walk away, to call Carrie Thomas tomorrow and tell her they'd just have to find another venue for the Day of the Dead festival, but I definitely didn't want to quit this early in the game.

There had to be a clue, something we were all missing. I just didn't know what it was yet.

"What about Mandy's family?" Max said. Clearly, he wasn't ready to give up, even though I felt as if we'd hit a dead end here.

"She was an only child," Evelyn replied. "Kind of a miracle baby, I guess—her mother had her when she was in her late thirties, which wasn't as common back then as it is now. Anyway, both her parents worshipped her, and were absolutely devastated when she died. Her mother passed away from ovarian cancer a year later. I played at her funeral service."

Tragedy piled on tragedy. No wonder the former cheerleader had turned into a bitter, vengeful ghost.

"That's your piano?" Max inquired, and Evelyn nodded.

"Yes," she said. "I still play at the Baptist church every week."

It was nice to hear that she still kept up with

her playing, but that wasn't really why we were here. "And Mandy's father?" I asked.

Evelyn's expression grew sorrowful. "He just sort of disappeared into his shell after Mandy's mom died. He kept his plumbing business going, but he didn't want to talk to anyone or interact with the community. He retired about ten years ago and sold the business."

"But he's here in Las Vegas?" Max inquired. He still looked interested and engaged, but I knew him well enough to guess that now he was just plugging away because he didn't know what else to do.

Max Sullivan had never been very good at quitting.

"Yes, he still lives here," Evelyn said, although now her expression looked almost wary. "But I don't think it's a good idea to talk to him about this. He's practically a hermit these days—has someone run his errands for him, doesn't talk to anyone."

Was Mandy's father hiding from the world because grief had consumed him...or were these more the actions of a guilty man? Was it possible that her own father had killed her?

As soon as that thought crossed my mind, I wanted to banish it to the farthest reaches of my brain. This was a man who'd lost his daughter to a terrible tragedy, and who'd lost his wife barely a year later. Just because I'd uncovered something truly horrible in the Moreno family's past didn't mean that every single male family member out there was motivated by the same awful impulses.

"Oh, we won't bother him," Max said hastily, obviously wanting to reassure Evelyn that we weren't about to descend on Mr. Carson's house and demand that he tell us everything he knew about his daughter's murder. "I was just wondering if there was anyone else here in town who could tell us more about Mandy."

Evelyn shook her head. "A lot of her old friends and classmates are still here, obviously, but I don't think there's anyone in Las Vegas who could tell you anything more than I have." She paused there. "Why is this so important now? Why did you want to know about that awful Bloody Mary game?"

Max and I had already agreed on the drive over here that it was probably better not to say that I'd had a direct conversation with Mandy's ghost. I supposed Evelyn might hear through the grapevine eventually that apparently I'd been communing with her spirit, but if she got that information from someone else, she could always dismiss it as gossip and nothing more.

Hearing it from the horse's mouth was an entirely different proposition.

"Someone mentioned the game to me," I said, which was true enough. "But also, I'd never heard about Mandy's death until recently, and since we're doing a Day of the Dead festival for the first time, I thought it might be nice to make a special *ofrenda* for her as a way of honoring her life."

Ofrendas were the altars families created for their dead loved ones to observe *El Día de los Muertos,* or the Day of the Dead. They could be set up on a table of their own, or placed on a piece of furniture that would accommodate the offerings of food and drink and flowers, of sugar skulls and any other mementos family members might think were appropriate. It was a way of honoring the memory of people who were no longer here by surrounding their images with the things they'd loved when they were alive. I'd thought about doing one for my grandmother but had realized she still didn't seem completely gone to me, not when I'd had a chance to communicate with her on the astral plane several times since her death. No, to me she felt more like a relative who'd simply moved to a different country, someone who might not have been in my life from day to day but was still definitely around.

Making an *ofrenda* for Mandy sounded a lot better than explaining that I had to solve her murder in the next day and a half, or the festival would be as much of a goner as she was.

At once, Evelyn's expression softened. "Oh, that would be wonderful," she said. "Of course, she had a lovely church service—the place was packed, not a single seat available ...and of course her parents had a beautiful marble headstone for her grave—but I've often thought it would have been better to have some kind of plaque or something else to mark the spot where she died, just so people would know to show the place the proper respect."

Pretty much the exact same thing Mandy wanted. No wonder the two of them had been besties back in the day.

"Why didn't they?" Max asked then. "Why try to sweep the whole thing under the rug?"

Although Evelyn could never look disapprovingly at her idol, something about the way she stiffened told me she also wasn't very happy about his question.

"I don't think anyone was trying to *hide* what happened," she said. "It was more that the mayor and the members of the city council decided it was better for the town to move on. It was very traumatic for everyone—I think an entire year went by before we girls felt safe walking someplace on our own, and I know my friends and I were always looking over our shoulders whenever we were out in public."

Which was pretty much what Deanne had told me her mother had said about the situation, when commenting on conversations she'd had with Evelyn. Not that I'd ever suspected the woman of lying about what had happened, but sometimes memories got blurred after so many years had passed.

And although we'd never had anything quite so traumatic to deal with lately—well, until Tom Gallegos' scheming younger brother had killed his sibling in the harvest festival's corn maze—I couldn't deny that I'd seen that same sort of mindset in city government more often than I would have liked. Everyone wanted everything to run smoothly, and putting down a plaque to show where a young girl had been brutally murdered wasn't exactly the sort of public image a town like mine wanted to present.

Once again, Max sent me a significant glance, and I allowed myself a tiny lift of my shoulders in reply. The whole thing left a nasty taste in my mouth, but that didn't mean some kind of skull-duggery was involved.

Well, except for what had happened in that quiet little spot between those two cottonwood trees.

"I really can't think of anything else," Evelyn said, obviously trying to fill the awkward silence that had just descended. "And I need to get dinner started."

That was a dismissal if I'd ever heard one. In unison, Max and I rose from the couch where we'd been sitting, and after an awkward pause, I said, "Thank you for taking the time to see us."

Evelyn also got up from her seat, expression now almost embarrassed, as if she'd just realized that her previous words had bordered on rude. "I'm not sure I helped all that much—"

"Oh, you did," Max cut in. He wore one of his famously dazzling smiles, though, so I doubted that she'd even noticed the way he'd interrupted her. "We learned a lot. Thanks again."

The two of us headed for the door after that and then made our way to the gravel driveway where Max had left his Bronco. I didn't look back, but I had a feeling that Evelyn had stood in the open doorway for a bit longer than she needed to, watching us go.

Because she wanted to feast her eyes on Max for as long as possible...or because she wanted to make sure we really were leaving and hadn't decided to snoop around her property?

I told myself that was silly. The woman was busy, and obviously needed to get dinner ready before her husband got home from work. Maybe I could have paused to contemplate the assumed gender roles of such a particular situation, although it was entirely possible Evelyn Hodge enjoyed cooking. After all, I loved to cook, too, although I was also happy to have Max barbecue for me when the weather allowed.

We both got into the Bronco. Neither of us said anything until we were on 7th Street, heading toward downtown so we could pick up University Avenue and drive east to Max's ranch on the other side of I-25.

"So...what did you think of that?" he asked at last.

"I'm not sure," I replied. "I got the feeling she wasn't telling us the complete story, but then, I'll admit I'm a suspicious person."

Max cracked a grin at my remark. "No, you're not," he said. "You believe in the good in people."

True, I'd been raised that way, and even though my childhood hadn't been picture-perfect—I was definitely the opposite of blonde, popular Mandy Carson—I'd always had people around me who'd watched over me and made sure I lived a safe, mainly trouble-free life. Even the murder and mayhem I'd witnessed—secondhand, mostly, but still—over the past year or so hadn't shaken my faith that most people were generally pretty nice.

"As for not telling the whole story...." Max let the words fade away, then shook his head. "I don't know. All that happened a long time ago. It's totally possible that she just doesn't remember everything."

I had to admit that made sense. No, at fifty-four or so, Evelyn Hodge definitely wasn't one foot in the retirement home or anything, but still, thirty-eight years was a long time to hold on to details, especially ones that had been pretty painful.

Like a lot of other people who'd experienced the same trauma, she'd just wanted to put the tragedy behind her and get on with her life.

A life that included Mandy's former boyfriend. I still thought that was kind of strange, but then, I'd be the first to admit that if Raylene Bryant—née Brown—had dropped dead back in high school, I would have been more than happy to provide a shoulder to Max to cry on...and a whole lot more, if possible.

"I suppose so," I said. "And I suppose it isn't so strange that she hadn't heard about the 'Bloody Mary' thing, either, since I'd never heard of it, either."

"Maybe it's something one of the kids themselves started," Max suggested. "It could be kind of a new thing. I could see someone overhearing a conversation about Mandy between their parents or whatever, and the kid decided to turn it into the local version of Bloody Mary."

"I could see that happening, too," I said. "And it would explain why neither Deanne nor I knew anything about it. Still...I'm not sure where to go from here."

Max lifted a hand from the wheel so he could reach over and squeeze one of mine where it rested on top of my purse, which was currently riding on my lap. "From here, we're going to my ranch so you can relax for a while. I know you think it's important to get this mystery solved, but the world isn't going to end if you don't."

No, I supposed it wouldn't...but at the same time, I didn't much like the idea of letting my hometown down, not to mention committing Mandy Carson to the eternal purgatory of staying stuck in Plaza Park because I couldn't figure out who'd come up behind her and throttled her in the dark.

If only she could have remembered something about her attacker, even their size relative to hers. She'd only said their hands were strong, which wasn't much to go on.

A football player would have powerful hands.

I told my brain to stop it, that the police had already determined decades ago that Jeff Hodge had a watertight alibi the night Mandy was killed. Whoever had done it, the murderer couldn't be Evelyn's husband.

My fingers wrapped themselves around Max's free hand, and I held on to him like that all the way back to his ranch. Just feeling his touch was enough to make me feel a little better about the situation...and I only perked up that much more when we entered the house and I breathed in the familiar, savory scent of his bodyguard Lou's famous mushroom pizza.

"How did you know I was craving exactly that?" I asked Max when we paused in the foyer so we could hang up our jackets in the coat closet.

"Just a feeling," he replied, a twinkle in his bright blue eyes.

We kissed then—just a fast one, because Lou called out from the kitchen, "Is that you, Max? I'm just about to put the pie on the table."

"Who else would it be?" Max responded, in a voice loud enough to carry from the spot where we stood to the back of the house where the kitchen was located. "Coming right in."

Apparently, Max had told Lou that this was a special evening of some sort, because all the candles on the sideboard and in the center of the table were lit, and some kind of soft jazz played in the background, drifting in through the built-in speakers that were installed in both the living and dining rooms.

I raised an eyebrow at Max as we went to take our usual seats, his at the head of the table and me at his right. "Is there some kind of occasion today I wasn't aware of?"

"Not really," Max replied smoothly. "I know you've been worried about this Mandy Carson thing, so I thought I'd give you a nice evening."

A very nice evening, considering he'd asked Lou to make me my favorite pizza, and a bottle of wine I knew Max couldn't have gotten anywhere here in Las Vegas was waiting in the marble caddy he used to prevent rings from marring the shining oak surface of the table. However, I wasn't able to comment on that, because Lou appeared, a gorgeous twelve-inch pizza pie balanced on a peel in one hand and a bowl of garden salad in the other.

"Need anything else, Max?" he asked.

"No, I think we're good," Max replied. "Thanks for putting all this together."

"Not a problem."

He headed back into the kitchen then, and Max reached for the bottle of wine, which had already been opened so it could air a bit. After pouring an inch or so into the heavy hand-blown glasses he always used, he handed one to me and then picked up the glass that had been sitting next to his own plate.

"To fixing the past," he said.

That sounded like a good toast to me. I touched my glass to his and sipped some of the wine. It was a fruity Washington pinot noir, not so bold that it would overpower the delicate flavors of the pizza.

"To fixing the past," I replied.

For a minute or so, we were both silent, sipping our wine, savoring the luscious flavors of mushroom sauteed in marsala wine and butter, and topping Lou's inimitable hand-tossed pizza crust. It was a lovely moment, in the warmly lit dining room with its local landscapes on the walls and the rustic, handcrafted furniture that fit the ranch house perfectly, but I still couldn't quite ignore the tick of the mantel clock in the next room, almost but not quite hidden beneath the music playing softly through the home's speaker system.

That clock was going to keep on ticking whether or not I made any headway in Mandy Carson's murder case.

"It's going to be okay," Max said quietly. "You're doing your best."

I set down my wine glass. "What if my best isn't good enough?"

In answer, he sent me a very direct look, those blue eyes of his piercing as laser beams. "Your best is always good enough, Skye. Never forget that."

Even though I'd met Max's eyes like this plenty of times before now, that sky-hued look never failed to make me very glad I was sitting down, just in case my traitor knees decided to give way.

"I'll try not to," I said, and he smiled.

"That's my girl."

We continued with our meal, each of us helping ourselves to another slice of pizza, and Max pouring an extra serving of wine. I had to admit that the more I drank, the more relaxed I felt, which could have been good or bad. With a pleasant buzz on like this, I didn't feel nearly as urgent about hunting down Mandy Carson's killer sometime in the next thirty-six hours.

But, as Max had pointed out, I was doing my best. If Carrie Thomas couldn't handle that, then it was on her.

Once it was obvious we'd eaten our fill, he excused himself so he could take the leftover pizza into the kitchen. A moment later, he returned, looking deadly serious.

"I have something I want to talk to you about," he said, and I lifted an eyebrow.

"Did you think of something we should have asked Evelyn Hodge?"

"No," Max replied, still wearing that solemn expression, as though he was back playing his Sam Howe character, the one who defused bombs and dangled from bridges while saving the world. "I thought of something I want to ask you."

And he opened his hand to reveal a robin's egg blue ring box.

Even I knew what that box meant, because not even a high-end jeweler in Santa Fe would have been good enough for him. No, he'd felt it necessary to go to Tiffany's for this all-important purchase.

My mouth went dry, and my heart began to thud in my chest. It was a good thing he was the one doing all the talking, because otherwise, I didn't know whether I would have been able to utter a rational sentence.

"Skye, you've been part of my life since forever," he said quietly, earnestly, his gaze locked on my face. "I want you to stay a part of my life for our next forever. You're my best friend, and my greatest love. Will you marry me?"

Words I'd dreamed of hearing for years and years. Words that, until a few months ago, I'd been pretty damn sure Max Sullivan would never say to me.

That was why I didn't even hesitate. Not for one second.

"Yes, Max," I said. "Yes, I'll marry you."

He pulled me to him, and we kissed, kissed so long that it took us a while to realize he'd never opened the box to reveal what was inside.

Not the standard solitaire engagement ring, that was for sure. No, instead the Tiffany's box contained a band of shimmering, perfect round-cut diamonds, each one probably at least a quarter carat in size. The only reason I could even hazard a guess as to their carat weight was that my grandmother Maureen's engagement ring's diamond had been about that big, a modest little stone that had been all my grandfather could afford.

As I stared down at the box, Max said...maybe not interpreting my stunned silence correctly, "I thought a big solitaire wasn't a very good idea, since you're always working in the kitchen. But if you want me to get you one—"

"No," I cut in. "This is perfect. I love it."

Wearing a relieved smile, he took the ring out of the box and slid it onto my finger. It fit perfectly, and I sent him a startled look. From what I'd read, rings that a man picked out without his girlfriend's input rarely fit on the first try.

"Deanne helped me," Max said, now wearing a sly smile. "She knew your ring size because she bought you that opal a couple of years ago for your birthday."

Yes, a lovely one set in silver, a ring I hardly ever wore because my October birthstone was fragile and I didn't dare risk it at the coffee shop.

"So...Deanne knew you were going to propose?" I asked, honestly astounded. Not because she wouldn't give Max any kind of help he needed for such a momentous occasion, but more that she'd been able to keep the secret all this time.

His eyes twinkled with amusement. "Yes. I swore her to secrecy, of course, and she did a wonderful job of keeping everything quiet."

"That's for sure," I replied. Usually, Deanne was a total chatterbox. It must have required a superhuman effort to make sure she kept her mouth shut so she wouldn't ruin the surprise.

"There's a second ring waiting for our wedding day," Max went on. "Then you can wear both of them together, but they still shouldn't get in the way."

I had to hope so. The ring was surprisingly comfortable on my finger, considering its carat weight, but two of them stacked together might be a different story.

Not that it mattered. I'd wear the biggest, flashiest diamond solitaire in the world if that was what he'd gotten me. But he hadn't, because, as usual, he'd been thinking of what would make me the most comfortable.

We kissed again...and again...and eventually made our commitment to one another even more real, even more solid, by slipping away to Max's bedroom. Several hours later, I was heading for home, all too aware of how late it was and how early I had to get up, even as I kept glancing at the flashing diamonds on my left hand, and wondering when I would get used to this amazing sensation.

I was going to be Max Sullivan's wife, and for now, that was more than enough to occupy my thoughts.

Mandy Carson would have to wait until tomorrow.

CHAPTER 7

Toys in the Attic

"I can't believe you didn't tell me," I said to Deanne the next morning.

She was practically grinning from ear to ear, clearly both thrilled that Max's and my engagement was real...and that he'd finally popped the question so she wouldn't have to keep the secret from me any longer.

"Oh, it took an extreme effort of will, that's for sure," she said. "But I promised Max, and you know I don't break my promises."

No, she didn't. She was the truest friend a person could ever have, and some days, I still wasn't sure how I'd gotten lucky enough to have her take me under her wing all those years ago when we were both just elementary school kids. She'd been the new girl in town back then, and, under most circumstances, our roles should have been reversed.

But she was pretty and popular almost from the beginning, while I'd always been the weird, dark, skinny kid with the family tragedy, someone none of my other classmates quite knew what to do with.

"But now you don't have to hide it," Deanne continued, with a significant glance at my left hand.

Not that I could have, even if I wanted to. The diamonds on that ring were so sparkly, I was pretty sure you could see them shining from space.

But even though I had to admit that being engaged to Max Sullivan was probably the best feeling in the world, I still had to get that morning's muffins and croissants and pastries in the oven.

So I went to work in the kitchen while Deanne headed out to the front of the shop to get everything ready for opening in less than an hour. Tilly, the talking cat who slept in the back room, had bolted through her door as soon as Deanne and I had hugged and squealed like a couple of high school kids when I flashed my new engagement ring at her. The cat might come back later today, or she might not, depending on how good her luck was in scrounging from the neighboring dumpsters that morning.

Since that was standard operating procedure for Tilly, I wasn't too worried about it. These days, she didn't come home with me very often, now that we knew the spell I'd cast to ensure she wouldn't talk around anyone except Max and Deanne and me seemed to be staying put and didn't show any signs of slipping. And because Tilly had been holding her own on the streets for years, I knew she was safe enough.

Our first couple of customers that morning were so focused on getting their daily shot of caffeine that they didn't seem to notice the glittering band of diamonds on my left hand. However, as soon as Lucy Margolis—my neighbor across the street and a regular customer—caught sight of the ring, she practically lunged for it, taking hold of my fingers so she could get a closer look.

"Is that what I think it is?" she demanded.

"Yes," I said, since I'd known all along that there was no way I'd be able to hide the change in Max's and my status. Sure, I could have just not worn the ring in public, but that would have defeated the purpose.

Honestly, I wanted people to know that Max and I were engaged.

"Oh, I'm so happy for you," Lucy said. Had her eyes turned just a little misty?

Maybe. After all, she'd known me my entire life, had been there to provide backup babysitting for my grandmother after my mother bailed on me at the tender age of two months and it became painfully obvious that my father was too lost in his own grief at being abandoned to step up and provide any kind of real parenting. To see me now engaged to one of the biggest movie stars in the world must have been some kind of real vindication.

"I wish your grandmother were here to see this," she went on. "She would be absolutely thrilled."

Most likely, yes. Although I'd done my best to conceal my crush on the handsome neighbor boy who'd been the most popular guy in town, my grandmother had been a very perceptive person. I had no doubt she knew exactly what my feelings were on the subject of Max Sullivan, even if she would never have embarrassed me by trying to talk to me about the situation.

"I wish she were here, too," I said, even as I felt the slightest stirrings of guilt. Not over getting engaged to Max—grandmother Maureen would have been happy to see me getting the one thing I wished for most in the world—but over the way I'd been talking to Mandy Carson. My grandmother had told me in no uncertain terms almost a year ago that I shouldn't be trying to commune with spirits, that I should stay in my lane and stick to tea leaf readings and having the occasional prophetic dream, and yet here I was, hanging around parks and talking to the ghost of a girl who'd been murdered almost forty years ago.

Not that it had done me a lot of good, considering the Day of the Dead festival was supposed to take place tomorrow, and I still didn't have the slightest clue as to who had come up behind Mandy all those years ago and wrapped their fingers around her neck, snuffing out her life before it had barely even begun.

Lucy gave a very small nod, looking sad. Although she was about fifteen years younger than my grandmother had been when she passed, the two women had always been fast friends, sharing recipes and gardening tips, doing their best to make sure I grew up happy and healthy, despite being an orphan. But then she seemed to perk up a bit, and asked, "When's the big day?"

Because Max and I already had discussed that subject the night before, I was ready to answer. "In April sometime. Max is going to be shooting a movie in January and February, so we wanted to make sure it was well after that in case the shoot goes long. We haven't settled on a date, though."

"Better make it late April," Lucy warned me, a thought that had already passed through my mind. Spring could be very late coming to New Mexico, and although even the end of April still wasn't a guarantee that the weather would cooperate, it definitely gave us more of a fighting chance.

"That's the plan," I told her. "I'm sure we'll get the date firmed up soon. But we just got engaged last night, so we haven't had a lot of time to figure everything out."

Lucy let out a happy breath. "It's just so wonderful," she said as I handed her a latte, her usual beverage of choice. "But now, I need to get going."

She sent me one last radiant smile, then hurried out. I watched her go, wearing a slight smile of my own...one that slipped a little as something occurred to me.

No, I'd never planned to hide my engagement. On the other hand, Lucy Margolis was one of Las Vegas's biggest gossips. I had no doubt that the story would make the rounds soon enough.

I told myself it was no big deal. After all, if Lucy was out there spreading the tale of Max's and my engagement, then it meant I might not have to keep repeating the story to every person I met.

Yes, that would be much better.

———

All the same, I couldn't quite cast off the sensation of foreboding that hung over me all the rest of the day. It was especially annoying because I knew I should be happy right now, that I should still be basking in the afterglow of Max's proposal.

It's just the clock ticking, I thought as I locked the back door to the shop and Deanne and I said goodbye. *You know you don't have much time left.*

There was the understatement of the century. The Day of the Dead festival was supposed to start at five o'clock tomorrow, and although Mandy had seemed quiescent the past couple of days, I had to believe that was only because no one had tried to replace the mural or do anything in the park that was remotely connected with the event. I was sure that as soon as someone appeared to re-install the mural or to start setting up pavilions for the various vendors, all hell would break loose.

Problem was, while I'd learned a few interesting bits and pieces from Evelyn, she definitely hadn't provided enough information for me to even begin formulating a theory as to who really had killed Mandy Carson.

I'd already made plans to get together with Max at my house, so I texted him when I got home to let him know he could come over whenever we wanted.

As usual, he was there within ten minutes of getting my message. The second he walked in the door, he took one look at my face and said, "That's not the expression of a woman who just got engaged."

"I'm sorry," I said at once, and meant both those words. "It's just that this whole Day of the

Dead thing is really giving me headaches. I know Carrie is counting on me to save the event, but I don't even know where to start. This would have been a lot easier if Mandy had started wreaking havoc in the park a couple of weeks ago. At least that way I would have had more time to get this figured out."

Immediately, Max came over and wrapped his arms around me so he could give me a comforting hug. After brushing a kiss on the top of my head, he replied, "Well, maybe there's something else we can do besides find Mandy's killer."

"Like what?" I asked plaintively. "She's pissed off that no one remembers her, and she's determined that no one else is going to get their day of remembrance, either."

Max's arms tightened around me for a second or two, and then he let go, face shining. "I've got it."

"Got what?" As far as I was concerned, there was no reason in the world for him to be looking so cheerful.

"The Day of the Dead is all about remembering lost loved ones, right?"

I nodded. "Yes. And?"

His grin didn't fade. If anything, it grew even brighter, making me wonder if I should reach in my purse for my sunglasses.

"Well, doesn't part of the celebration involve

people putting up those altars for the people they're honoring?"

For a second or two, I stared back at him. Then the import of his words sank in. After all, his suggestion wasn't so very different from my idea that a plaque should have been placed in the park to let the world know her life had been cut short there.

"So...you think if we put up an *ofrenda* for Mandy, then maybe we can get her to back off?"

"It's a start," he said. "Maybe you can tell her it's not like you're giving up trying to find her killer, but that you want to show her that people really do still remember her. That way, you can gain a little breathing space."

This all sounded like a brilliant idea...if she went for it.

Well, no time to find out like the present.

"Do you mind hanging out here for a bit?" I asked him. "I'm going to head over to the park and see what Mandy thinks of our idea."

One of Max's eyebrows lifted the slightest bit. "You don't want me to come along?"

Of course I would like to have him with me. Problem was, I didn't know whether his presence would scare Mandy off, and with time ticking inexorably down, I didn't think we could afford any further delays.

"I want you to," I responded, then hurried to

add, "but I'm not sure it's the best idea. Mandy seems kind of skittish."

No huge surprise for someone who'd been strangled by a faceless stranger.

To my relief, Max only gave a thoughtful nod. "Right. I hadn't thought of that. Then I'll just wait for you here."

I gave him a relieved kiss, then grabbed my purse and hurried out. Luckily, he'd parked on the street in front of the house and not in the driveway, like he sometimes did when we both knew we'd be staying in for the evening, so I was able to back out of the driveway without having to stop and ask him to move his SUV.

The day was a dark, lowering sort of one, with heavy gray skies but no rain. Just a cold, sharp wind that came from the north and shook loose the last brave leaves that still clung stubbornly to their branches.

It really wasn't the kind of day that seemed terribly ideal for meeting a ghost.

On the other hand, the gloomy weather seemed to have driven everyone out of the park, or maybe the news had spread that something hostile was lurking on its south side. Either way, I was very glad to find the place utterly deserted and know that I probably wouldn't have an audience for this latest interview. Even the ice cream shop across the street had its doors shut against the bitter wind, although

I noticed the neon "Open" sign still glowed in the front window.

Good enough.

Because the park was so empty, I could park nearby what I'd begun to think of as Mandy's clearing, even though it was really just a space between two trees. Yellow cottonwood leaves crunched underfoot as I crossed to the place where I'd spoken to her just the day before yesterday, and I got the uncomfortable feeling that she wasn't here, that she'd headed over to the Plaza to hang out with Byron T.'s ghost and catch up on the town's latest otherworldly gossip.

Okay, I didn't really think it worked like that.

Honestly, I wasn't sure how any of this worked. I was flying blind and just praying I'd be able to muddle through and come out the other side with the Day of the Dead festival saved and Mandy's killer in police custody.

Nice fantasy, but I knew I needed to take this one step at a time.

"Mandy?" I called out, knowing how tentative my voice sounded.

No response, except the wind rattling the bare branches overhead.

I paused to look around. A car—an older-model white Toyota—slowly made its way along the street as it looped around the park, but I doubted its driver could even see me where I stood, with the thick trunks of the trees blocking me from any casual observers.

"Mandy?" I said again.

This time she faded into existence, standing a few feet away from me. Just like last time, she appeared in shades of gray and in the same outfit of slouchy sweater, leg warmers, and that ridiculous polka-dot miniskirt. It made me think of a meme I saw once, one that said you needed to be careful about how you dressed each morning, because you might just end up wearing those same clothes for all eternity.

With my luck, I'd be stuck in one of my black tops and faded jeans until the end of time, since that was my usual uniform.

"Did you find out who killed me?" Mandy asked.

"No," I replied, and immediately, she frowned.

"Then why are you coming around here and bugging me?"

"Because I had an idea," I replied, hoping that Max wouldn't mind me appropriating his notion as my own, especially since we'd both been thinking along the same lines, anyway. I'd only done so because I didn't want to waste time trying to explain who he was. "I know you're upset because you think no one remembers you, that no one has gone to any trouble to honor your existence. So...what if I make you an *ofrenda* at the Day of the Dead festival?"

Her pale gray brows pulled together. "What's an *ofrenda*?"

"It's a kind of altar," I explained. "I'll put a picture of you on there, and it'll have flowers and your favorite foods, and I'll put lit candles along with the other offerings to commemorate your life."

"It sounds kind of pretty," she said, although she continued to frown and her tone was grudging at best. "But I'm supposed to be okay with a couple of flowers instead of you finding my killer?"

"No, no," I said hastily. "This is just to show you that you're remembered. I'll keep looking for the person who did this to you, I promise. But if there's no Day of the Dead festival, then I can't make an *ofrenda* for you."

This wasn't strictly true, obviously. I could have put together an altar at my own house anytime I wanted. But if Mandy thought that the only way she'd get such an offering was if the event was actually held, then I had a much better chance of her relenting.

Which turned out to be the case, because she nodded slowly, then said, "Okay. I like the idea of an *ofrenda*. But this doesn't get you off the hook. There are plenty of other events at this park I can mess with if you don't find the person who killed me."

Not an idle threat, because we had the Winter Wonderland festival the second week of December, and then farmer's markets May through the end of September. Any one of those would give Mandy ample opportunity to cause all kinds of havoc.

"I have no intention of giving up," I declared. "And you can ask some of the other ghosts in town if you need to know anything more about my track record when it comes to finding murderers."

"Oh, Mr. Wells already told me," Mandy replied. "Otherwise, I wouldn't have even bothered to give you this much time. But he said you were good at this stuff, which is why I gave you a chance."

Ol' Byron T. to the rescue, it seemed. Thank goodness he seemed to be looking out for me—or maybe he was just more interested in making sure everything went smoothly in our town.

"Well, thanks for that," I said. "Then we can go ahead with the Day of the Dead festival?"

A long pause. Mandy tapped a finger against her lip, a finger whose nail would be eternally decorated with chipped nail polish that I thought had once been bright pink. "Sure," she replied. "My favorite foods were ham and pineapple pizza and those maple bars you can get at O's Donuts."

Thank God O's was still in business, or I might

have been scrambling to find that one particular item. Somehow, I doubted this demanding ghost would have been too happy with any substitutions. And I wouldn't even comment on the pineapple pizza, because I didn't want to piss her off.

"Done," I said. "You'll have the best *ofrenda* at the whole festival."

This seemed to be all the reassurance she needed, because she promptly winked out of existence.

I glanced around, but no one seemed to have been anywhere near us during that entire exchange. While it seemed a little too early to breathe a sigh of relief, I had to admit I was feeling a lot better than I had even five minutes earlier.

I got my phone out of my purse. Four twenty-two, early enough that I guessed Carrie would still be at work. Because I'd already entered her contact information on my phone, it only took a minute for the call to go through.

"Hi, Carrie," I said cheerfully. "It looks like the Day of the Dead festival is a go."

CHAPTER 8

Earned Offerings

"This is a miracle," Carrie Thomas breathed as she looked at the organized chaos all around us.

Privately, I had to admit it did seem kind of miraculous that the Day of the Dead festival was happening after all. I'd come to the park this morning to meet Carrie and let her know where I wanted to set up my *ofrenda,* and when I arrived, it was to find more than a dozen workmen and volunteers rebuilding the marigold mural and setting up the various pavilions that the vendors would occupy.

The place for the *ofrendas* was being erected near the mural, and really wasn't much more than lots of long tables with weatherproof vinyl covering them. The table space was separated into little squares about eighteen inches across, not as much room as I'd hoped I would have.

Well, I'd just have to make it work.

"I'm surprised you could get all these people here on such short notice," I told Carrie, and she gave a pleased little tilt of her head.

"Oh, I had everyone on standby, just in case," she replied. She wasn't quite smiling, but I could tell she was very, very relieved that this was going to happen after all. "How did you manage to do it?"

"Just a promise," I said, and left it at that. "And it's okay for me to have this space?"

I pointed at the square next to where we stood, one I'd chosen because it was far away from the mural—better safe than sorry—but provided a good view of the two trees that Mandy seemed to have made her eternal hangout.

"After what you did to make this happen, you can have any space you want," Carrie told me. "You can come back after two to set it up. The festival itself won't start until five."

Which I'd already known, but still, it was something of a relief to realize I still had time to gather all my supplies. I'd gone to O's earlier this morning to pick up one of Mandy's beloved maple bars, but obviously, none of the pizza places were open at this time of the morning. It was too late in the season to provide flowers from my own garden, which might have been a nice touch, but I'd stopped at my favorite local florist after going to the donut shop so I could buy pink roses for the altar.

The one thing that had stumped me was a photo of Mandy. At dinner the night before, Max had suggested that maybe we could clip one of the pictures we'd seen in the newspapers at the historical society, but defacing the society's archives didn't sound like a very good idea. I'd only told him I'd figure something out, even if it meant printing one of the grainy photos I'd found of her online.

Now, though, as I visualized the *ofrenda* in my mind, I realized that wouldn't work at all. I was going to do everything I could to make the altar look as lovely as possible, and that meant we had to have a good picture of Mandy, maybe a school portrait or something like that.

And right now, I could think of only one person who might have something like that.

Andrew Carson.

I'd already looked up his information, ignoring how Evelyn Hodge had told Max and me that we needed to leave him alone. Mr. Carson lived in a house not too far from mine—in fact, I'd probably driven past it dozens of times without even knowing who lived there.

Not that I would have known there any special significance about that one particular home.

It wasn't until Mandy had made her presence known that I'd even realized a high school girl had been killed in the park where I'd spent so many hours of my life.

"Perfect," I told Carrie. "I'll be back after two."

And that meant I had plenty of time to run this one particular errand.

Andrew Carson's home was a two-story farmhouse not all that unlike mine, although his was pale green with dark green trim, rather than white and blue. And it was meticulously maintained, no peeling paint, no weeds in the yard.

For some reason, this surprised me. Evelyn had described Mandy's father as being practically a hermit, and I'd just sort of imagined him living in a ramshackle house like something out of *Grey Gardens* or whatever.

But then I realized that he'd probably focused on keeping up the house and its yard so he wouldn't have to think about all the losses he'd suffered in his life.

Unlike my front walk, Andrew Carson's wasn't covered in leaves. I swept mine on the weekend but simply didn't have the time to take care of it during the week, while it looked as though he must come out here and clear it every single day.

As I headed up the front steps, I could feel my heart start to pound a little. Maybe it was stupid to be handling this on my own, but Max had a Zoom call with some producers this morning and I hadn't wanted to wait.

Besides, I got the feeling Mr. Carson wasn't the sort of person who liked to be ganged up on, and might not feel as threatened by one woman coming here by herself.

Before I could lose my nerve, I reached out to touch the little button next to the front door. No Ring doorbell here; a normal *ding-dong* sounded from somewhere inside the house, followed by silence.

I waited on the front porch, feeling my unease ratchet upward with every passing second. Despite Evelyn's claim that Andrew Carson never went anywhere, I couldn't help worrying that maybe he really had gone out today, had run over to the hardware or grocery store for some necessary item that he didn't want to wait for.

If that turned out to be the case, I wasn't sure what I should do next. Lie here in wait and hope he'd return eventually? Leave a note?

But then the door opened, and a tall, thin man who looked like he was in his middle or late sixties stared out at me. His hair was iron gray, telling me it had probably been dark brown when he was younger, and his eyes were a startling light blue under their heavy brows.

"What do you want?"

Not the friendliest greeting in the world, but then again, I hadn't really expected to be welcomed with open arms.

"I want to talk to you about your daughter," I said simply.

His eyes narrowed. "My daughter is dead."

Four words that probably would have flummoxed most people. I stood my ground, however, and said, "I know. But I just talked to her ten minutes ago."

He didn't move, only stood there and continued to fix me with that steely stare. Then he said, his tone flat, "Is this a joke?"

"No," I replied. "I want to make an *ofrenda* for Mandy at the Day of the Dead festival. She told me her favorite foods were Hawaiian pizza and the maple bars from O's."

A tremor went through Andrew Carson's lean form. "How could you know that?"

"Because she told me," I said simply.

A long pause, one that made me fear he was going to slam the door in my face. But then he said, "I think you'd better come inside."

He opened the door and stepped out of the way so I could enter the house. Unlike my own place, which didn't have much of an entry, the

Carson home had a real foyer with a coat closet to one side and a little table placed up against the wall next to the stairs. To our left was what looked like the living room, and Andrew Carson gestured in that direction.

"We can sit in there."

I followed him into the room and sat down on the couch he'd indicated. As far as I could tell, the whole place looked as though it had been frozen in some kind of time capsule, with Laura Ashley–inspired chintz on the windows and sofa and matching chairs. It all looked extremely fussy, and entirely unlike a home where a man lived alone.

But his wife probably did all the decorating, I thought. *And then after both she and Mandy were gone, he didn't want to change anything.*

Mr. Carson sat down on one of the chairs that faced the couch, expression still grim. "You're that girl, aren't you."

It wasn't framed as a question, but I answered it anyway. "The one who solves murders? Yes, that's me."

"No," he said roughly. "The one who talks to ghosts."

For someone who didn't get out much, it appeared Andrew Carson still heard a lot of the local gossip. "I do a little of both," I admitted.

"And you claim to have talked to my daughter."

"I'm not 'claiming' anything," I told him. "I

really have spoken to her, twice. Her spirit seems to mostly hang around in the park."

Those words made Mr. Carson wince slightly, and I wished I could have taken them back. Even after all these years, he wouldn't want to be reminded of the place where his daughter had been brutally killed.

"What did she want?" he asked then, his voice dropping to nearly a murmur.

"To be remembered," I said softly. "That's why I'm making an *ofrenda* for her. But I also want to find out who really killed her."

"No one knows," Andrew Carson said. "The police were never able to find anything."

"I know," I replied. "Evelyn Hodge told me about it. Still, cold cases get solved all the time. I want to try."

The mention of Evelyn's name made him shake his head. "That poor kid," he said, surprising me. His gruff appearance gave the impression of someone who had little concern for others. "She was really shaken up by the whole thing."

I nodded. "Yes, I could tell she still gets upset when she has to talk about losing her best friend. I honestly can't even imagine."

And didn't want to. Deanne was my rock, the person who'd always been there for me ever since we were both around seven years old. Losing her in such a terrible way would be utterly devastating.

"So...you spoke with Mandy."

"Yes," I said. "She was really upset about the Day of the Dead festival, but I managed to talk her down by telling her I'd make an altar for her...and also promising to find her killer."

One of Andrew Carson's gray-frosted brows lifted slightly. "And you really think you'll be able to do that?"

"I hope so," I replied. For a moment, I hesitated, wondering whether I should say anything else, but then told myself this probably wasn't the time for false modesty, not when I had a pretty decent track record for this sort of thing. "I mean, I've done a better job of it lately than the police."

Was that a hint of a smile at the corner of his stern mouth? I thought maybe it was, although something about the expression seemed almost rusty, as if he hadn't had much reason to smile for many years.

Not that I could blame him.

"I wish I could help you," he said, that ghost of a smile disappearing as if it had never been. "But I told the police everything I knew, which wasn't much. Mandy didn't go with the rest of the cheerleading squad to the big Estancia game because she was behind in her U.S. History class, and the teacher had warned her she was going to get a D on her quarter report card if she didn't get an A on her midterm. She stayed here and went to the library to study because she said she could concentrate better there."

I nodded, but didn't say anything. Some of this I'd already seen in the newspaper clippings Max and I had found at the historical society, but the story felt entirely different when told by the man who'd lost his daughter that night.

Voice heavy with a grief and regret that hadn't abated, even over almost forty years, Andrew went on, "I offered to drive her, but she said she could walk home when she was done, that it wasn't that far."

It felt kind of far to me—the public library, which was located in a gorgeous Greek Revival–style building and which had been constructed thanks to a grant from Andrew Carnegie himself—was probably about half a mile from the Carson house, give or take, but that still seemed like kind of a long walk, especially after dark.

But Las Vegas was generally a safe place even now, and back in the 1980s, had been safer still. I had a feeling Mandy had never thought when she set out after her study session that she would never make it home.

"When it got to be past nine-thirty, I started to worry," Andrew continued. "Even if she'd stayed at the library all the way until closing time at nine, she should have still made it home by then. I got in my car to drive around and look for her—

Mandy's mom was already bed-ridden by then and had to stay home—and then when I saw all those cop cars and flashing lights over by the park, I knew."

"I'm so sorry," I murmured, even as I realized how inadequate those words were. Having to deal with the death of your only child was tragic enough, but going through that kind of ordeal while your wife was dying of cancer?

Absolutely horrible.

Andrew's fingers tightened on the knees of his worn corduroy pants, but I noticed he didn't try to brush me off with the usual "it's fine" or "it's been a long time" or whatever else people tended to say when they were attempting to blunt the edges of a trauma they'd suffered.

"They could never figure out who did it," he said. "And eventually...well, I won't say I didn't stop thinking about it, but at least it wasn't every second of every day." He straightened then and gave me a very keen look. "But I get the feeling you didn't come here to listen to me tell old stories."

"Well, not exactly," I confessed. "Although now I know a couple of things I didn't know before, so it might help. What I really wanted, though, was a picture of Mandy. For the *ofrenda*," I added hastily, in case he might think I was some weirdo who collected the high school pictures of murder victims. "It's kind of traditional to put a photo on the altar, and I don't have anything I can really use."

I'd halfway expected Andrew to offer some kind of protest, but he just nodded. "Sure," he said. "Give me a minute."

He got up from the chair where he was sitting and walked down the hall, presumably going to one of the home's bedrooms. For the first time, I noticed there weren't any photos at all in the living room where I sat, nothing to indicate that he'd once shared this house with his family. Had it been too painful for him to look at those reminders of his loss, or did he just not want any visitors to see them and ask questions he didn't want to answer?

Obviously, I wouldn't ask.

A moment later, he returned with a large gilt-framed portrait in his hands. "This was Mandy's picture from junior year," he said as he handed it over. "She was so happy with the way it turned out."

As I took it from him and looked down at the photo, I could see why she'd been proud of the portrait. A lot of high school pictures were awkward at best and downright mortifying at their worst, but Mandy's was almost elegant. She wore a simple black top and gold hoop earrings, and she'd curled her hair—not frizzy 1980s curls, but just enough to give her straight locks some wave and body. In fact, she could have stood in for Amanda

Seyfreid's younger sister...if Amanda had been alive back in 1985, of course.

"This is lovely," I said, and meant it. Although I could tell even from her gray-scale ghost form that Mandy had been a very pretty girl, there was no way for me to have known that her eyes were a perfect aquamarine blue, or that her pale hair had had the slightest hint of soft gold.

To be perfectly honest, she was the kind of girl I would have been bitterly jealous of back in high school, although even then I'd known deep down it was stupid to be envious of someone just because they'd had better luck in the genetic lottery than I did. And really, even though it had taken me a while to grow into them, I was now pretty happy with my looks...most days, anyway.

"She was a beautiful girl," Andrew said, and his mouth tightened. "Took after her mother, luckily."

I wouldn't comment on that, since I'd never seen a picture of her. And although time had worn heavily on Mr. Carson, the bones of his face were chiseled, very refined, and I guessed he had been quite attractive back in the day.

"The picture will be perfect for Mandy's *ofrenda*," I said. "I'll take very good care of it, and I'll bring it back tomorrow after I take down the altar."

He nodded. "That will work."

Hesitantly, I said, "Will you come to the event and see her altar? I think she'd like it."

A very long pause. Then he replied, "No, I don't think so."

No clarification as to why, and I didn't press him. Maybe it was only that seeing her *ofrenda* would remind him all over again of his loss, and that was the last thing I wanted to do.

So I only murmured a thank-you, and rose from the couch, the picture still in my hand. Mr. Carson didn't offer to see me out, but I didn't mind.

I knew the way.

It was a good thing that Levitation Latte wasn't open on Saturday, because between getting a slice of Hawaiian pizza for the altar and then running home when I realized I'd forgotten the vanilla-scented candle and its matching black metal base, putting together Mandy's *ofrenda* took more time out of my day than I'd thought it would.

Luckily, everyone else was busy getting their own altars set up, most of them with framed photos like mine and votive candles and flowers. Marigolds, bright and cheerful, seemed to be the most popular choices, probably because they were the signature flower of the original Mexican festival, and were a lovely complement to the few golden leaves that remained on the park's cottonwood trees, although I also saw plenty of roses and other blooms as well.

The entire site buzzed with activity right until the time the festivities were supposed to start at five. I had a feeling Carrie Thomas hadn't really planned it that way, but because so much had been put off until the last minute for fear Mandy's ghost would show up and wreak havoc, they were way behind schedule.

However, once everyone was finished with their setup—completed at a quarter 'til, which probably hadn't done much for Carrie's blood pressure—you would never have been able to tell that it wasn't meant to happen this way. All the altars were in place, all the vendors set up in their various pop-up pavilions, and a mariachi band who'd traveled from Santa Fe was already playing in the bandstand a few yards away from the spot where the *ofrendas* were located.

People gravitated toward the marigold mural first, probably figuring they should pay their respects there before moving deeper into the display of *ofrendas* and the row of vendors. I looked around, wondering if Mandy was going to make an appearance so she could inspect her altar, but I didn't see any sign of her.

Maybe the crowds of people had scared her off.

But Max was there, approaching the altar I'd just set up, with Deanne and her husband Mike at his side. As soon as they were close enough to really see what I'd done, Max said, "That looks amazing, Skye."

"Thanks," I said, and smiled as he leaned across the table so he could give me a kiss on the cheek. Nothing too passionate—a full-on lip lock while surrounded by altars dedicated to loved ones who'd passed wouldn't have been very appropriate—and yet, familiar warmth flooded through me. You'd think I'd have been used to Max's caresses by now, but apparently not.

"Where did you get the picture?" Deanne asked, also coming closer so she could inspect the arrangement of pink roses and blue hydrangeas, clustered to make a frame of its own around the portrait Andrew Carson had given me.

"From Amanda's father," I replied, and Deanne gave me a shocked look.

"You went and talked to him?"

"I did," I said. Max and Mike looked curious as well, so I added, "He was actually really nice. Sad, obviously, but he didn't mind talking to me and telling me a few things I didn't know. And he let me borrow the picture. I need to take it back tomorrow."

"How long do you leave the altars up?" Mike inquired.

"Overnight," I replied. "But I'm going to take the valuable stuff home with me. I mean, I doubt someone would come along and steal Mandy's photo, but I don't want to take that chance. Her father doesn't have a whole lot left of her."

That comment sobered everyone for a moment...but then Max's eyes got that familiar twinkle.

"So, Hawaiian pizza was her favorite?"

"Yes," I said severely, hoping my tone would tell him I wouldn't countenance any jokes at Mandy's expense. "That's why there's a piece of it on the altar."

Max's mouth twitched slightly at my response, but it was Mike who spoke next. "Well, I'd be happy to relieve you of that maple bar if you're going to toss it by the end of the evening."

"It'll probably be pretty stale by then," Deanne told him. "I have a better idea—let's get some churros."

That sounded like a great idea to me. Yes, we'd probably end up getting tacos from the truck that had parked at the end of the row of vendors, but something sweet and cinnamon-y would be perfect to tide me over until then.

Because it wasn't as though I had to stay by the altar, I went along with my friends and wandered through the vendors, eating a churro and listening to the music from the mariachi band drift across the park. It didn't seem as if this event was quite as well attended as the town's harvest festival, but that was probably because things had been up in the air until almost the last minute.

Still, I guessed at least a thousand people had turned out to see the *ofrendas* and sign the mural, sometimes with just a signature and sometimes with their messages adorned with hearts and flowers and sketches of sugar skulls, and also to watch when the fire dancers in their gorgeous traditional Mexican costumes came out after it was full dark. From time to time, I'd wander past Mandy's *ofrenda,* just to make sure no one had touched anything, but it seemed to be fine.

The festivities were scheduled to be over promptly at nine o'clock. Most of the crowd drifted away then, heading back to their cars—or to their homes if they were in walking distance—although those of us who had *ofrendas* to dismantle went to begin taking them down. Mike and Deanne left around then, although Max stayed behind, saying he wanted to help me with Mandy's altar.

Honestly, there wasn't that much to do, but I got it. He wanted to stay with me, and hoped the evening wouldn't end here.

Which was fine. I was feeling a little more tired than I usually would have on a Saturday night, but chalked that up to all the running around I'd done earlier in the day. Just as I was reaching for the pizza slice on the altar so I could throw it in the trash, I froze.

There was Mandy, standing a few feet away. Her head was tilted to one side, and she wore a small smile.

"I like it," she said.

Luckily, no one was nearby except Max—the people who'd set up altars on either side of me had already packed their things and left—and he was used to this sort of thing.

Kind of.

"I'm glad you were able to see it," I replied. "I looked around, but I didn't see you earlier."

Next to me, Max froze. In an undertone, he said, "She's here?"

"Yes," I told him. "Standing over there. You don't see her?"

He shook his head.

Interesting. Was it that Max wasn't capable of seeing ghosts, or just that Mandy had decided she only wanted me to catch a glimpse of her?

"No, he can't see me," Mandy said. Her voice carried to me clearly, but since Max didn't react, I knew those words had reached my ears alone. "No one can...except you."

I supposed that made sense. Otherwise, there should have been tons of reports of seeing a spectral girl at Plaza Park over the years. Exactly why I could speak with her and see her as clearly as any other person, I didn't know, especially since Max had been able to perceive the presence of the little ghost girl in the basement of the hotel just across the street.

"Why can't he?" I asked, and Mandy shrugged.

"I don't know," she said. "It's always been like that for me. I know some of the other ghosts let people see them every once in a while, but no one's ever been able to tell I was here...except you."

Well, I'd leave that question for another day. I supposed if I got curious enough, I could reach out to Mason Fowles, an Arizona-based ghost hunter I'd met while trying to solve the mystery of the paranormal investigator Calum McRae's untimely death. I'd have to be really dying for answers, though, because Mason was probably one of the most unpleasant people I'd ever met, and I really didn't want to deal with him again unless I absolutely had to.

"Did my dad give you that picture?" Mandy asked next, tilting her head toward the gold-framed 8x10 photo on the altar.

"Yes," I said. "But I'm going to bring it home with me tonight to keep it safe, then take it back to him tomorrow."

"I'm glad he let you borrow it," she replied. A shadow moved across her face, and she asked, "Was he sad?"

As much as I wanted to tell her Andrew Carson was doing okay, I knew that would have been a lie. "Yes, he was sad," I said. "You haven't been able to visit him?"

Mandy shook her pale head. "No. Whenever I try to go to my house, it's like I trip over the curb or something, and then end up right back in the park. I can go to other places in Las Vegas, but not home."

Interesting. Did all ghosts have spots that were interdicted for some reason, or was there something else going on here?

Once again, I had no idea. To be honest, what I didn't know about ghosts and hauntings would have filled an encyclopedia.

"He was nice to me, though," I told her. "And he was okay with letting me borrow the picture, which made all the difference on your *ofrenda*."

Mandy's expression grew wistful. "I wish I could've eaten the pizza."

I wished she could have, too. Mike had spirited away the maple bar over Deanne's protests, but the pizza was destined to go into the trash once I was done here. "It looked good," I said, glad my tone was neutral.

She came closer and passed a hand over the altar, although I noticed how she took care to keep some distance between her ghostly fingers and the items on the tabletop. I got the feeling that she knew her hand would pass right through them, and was being careful not to remind herself of her current incorporeal state.

Her expression seemed to harden, and she said, "Okay, you had your little dead-guy party. Now it's time to find out who killed me. Work fast."

After delivering that ultimatum, she disappeared. I blinked, and Max moved for the first time since Mandy had appeared, coming closer to me.

"What happened?" he murmured, and I let out a breath.

"Party's over," I said. "Now I need to get back to work."

CHAPTER 9

School Daze

Max ended up staying the night at my place. We both had toiletries and spare clothes stashed at each other's homes, just so we'd have the necessities available no matter where we slept. Hovering in the back of my mind was the uneasy realization that eventually we'd have to sit down and really talk about what we planned to do about our domestic arrangements in the future, since once we were married, it wasn't as though we could keep on living in separate houses.

And all right, I'd heard of celebrity couples who did that very thing, but I was old-fashioned enough to believe that I should share a roof with the man I'd married.

However, since we hadn't set a date yet, I figured we could go along like this for a few more months before we really had to hammer out some logistics.

It was wonderful to have Max there that morning, though, to know I really didn't have to do much today except some laundry...and go back to Mr. Carson's house so I could return Mandy's picture to him.

We went into the kitchen, where I got to work mixing up buttermilk pancakes and frying some bacon. I did it the same way my grandmother had taught me, by using her old cast-iron pan, the one we used to joke we could use for self-defense in case anyone ever tried to break into the house.

Max wasn't sitting idle, though. He could brew a pretty mean batch of coffee, and he went ahead and poured some beans into the grinder, then busied himself getting that morning's pot of mocha java going. Soon enough, the rich scent of coffee blended with the wonderful aroma of the applewood-smoked bacon, and I found myself breathing it in, wishing every day could start out like this.

Well, except without an apparently unsolvable murder hanging over my head.

"What's on the docket for today?" Max asked as he handed me my cup of coffee.

I took a sip, flipped some bacon, and decided the timing was right to get started with the pancakes. Since I'd already set out the electric griddle and heated it up, all I had to do was start pouring the batter.

"I need to return Mandy's photo," I said, and picked up the big quart-sized yellow measuring cup I used for pancakes, then started dripping it onto the hot griddle. "After that, some laundry."

He chuckled. "You really lead an exciting life, don't you?"

I shot a grin at him, then went on my toes so I could land a healthy smack on his cheek. "You know me—I'm a real daredevil."

After taking a sip from the cup he held, he said, "I like you that way. It's refreshing."

I enjoyed being "refreshing," so I didn't argue. However, I could feel my smile fading as I said, "What I really need to be doing is working on this damn murder case. Problem is, I have absolutely no idea what I'm supposed to do next. If there were any leads once upon a time, they're definitely nowhere to be found now. And Mandy definitely made it sound as though she'd be more than happy to get up to all kinds of mischief if I don't get this solved soon."

"Considering what she did to the first marigold mural, I'm not surprised," Max observed dryly. "But we'll figure something out."

He said "we" so confidently, as if he was just as bound to finding a solution as I was. I didn't bother to argue, because I knew how much help he'd been in the past, how much support he'd given me. While the current situation certainly felt hopeless, I wouldn't let myself give up. Possibilities always managed to present themselves when you had Max Sullivan at your side.

"There has to be something the police overlooked," I said as I flipped pancakes. "Some kind of clue that didn't seem important at the time."

"Maybe," Max replied. "Too bad we can't take a look at their files."

If they even still existed. Yes, I'd read accounts of the FBI solving cases twenty or thirty years or more after the original crime occurred, but it didn't sound as if the FBI had been involved in Mandy's murder, for whatever reason.

It couldn't hurt to ask, though.

"Would the FBI have been involved?" I inquired, and Max immediately shook his head.

"No, the FBI usually doesn't have jurisdiction in a regular homicide. This murder didn't happen on federal property, and it doesn't sound as if the local police ever even identified a suspect, someone who would have gone on the run. That's also a case where the FBI could get involved. But a regular local murder?" His shoulders lifted, and he sipped some more coffee. "There wouldn't have been any reason for them to be here."

I stared at him, a little startled by the wealth of

information that had just sprung from his lips. "You know an awful lot about it."

Another one of his wide grins, this one even more incandescent because of its contrast to the dull, gray morning outside. "Oh, well...I did a lot of research for my cop roles, so I ended up learning a bunch about how all this stuff works. I know TV and movies make it seem as if the FBI is involved in murder cases all the time, but it's a lot rarer than you might think."

So much for that idea.

"But the local police would still have all the files connected to Mandy's murder," he went on. "There's no statute of limitations on murder, so they have to keep that information, even when a case is stone cold."

"But we both know Chief DeVargas isn't going to let us look at any of them," I said, and picked up my tongs so I could shuffle the bacon around to make sure it was all cooking evenly. Luckily, it was getting close, as were the pancakes, so I knew we'd be sitting down to eat soon.

This time, Max didn't smile. "I doubt it. I mean, I could try going to talk to her, turn on the charm, but I have a feeling she's immune."

He was probably right. I knew my fiancé's smile made me swoony every time he turned it on me, but Marie DeVargas was made of sterner stuff.

I didn't exactly sigh, but I was glad that I had

the distraction of dishing up the pancakes and bacon to keep me from getting too depressed over the situation. With hardly any evidence to go on and a trail that was decades old, how in the world was I supposed to solve this crime before Mandy went on the rampage again?

Max must have noticed the shift in my expression, because he took the plate of bacon from me, kissed me on the cheek, and said, "It's going to be fine. Now that the Day of the Dead festival is behind you, maybe it's time to get out your tea leaves and see if they have anything they can tell you."

He was probably right. I'd been so busy that I hadn't been in the right mental place to do a reading, but it seemed like the logical next step.

Also....

"If I do a tea-leaf reading, I'm going to have to kick you out," I warned him.

He only smiled. "I figured you were going to do that anyway once you got started with the laundry. It's okay. Margaret sent me a bunch of scripts Friday afternoon, and I really need to crack them open and see if any of them look interesting."

Margaret was Max's agent, a not-very-friendly woman who had never seemed to approve of me, or my relationship with Max. Luckily, while he might have taken her advice when it came to signing onto various film projects, he clearly didn't pay any attention to her opinions on his personal life.

And even though I knew making movies was his life—and the way he earned those eight figures per film—I always experienced a mental wince when he talked about looking at scripts or having contract meetings. All it meant to me was that he'd be gone for weeks or months, and I'd have to muddle along without him by my side.

Which you'll do without complaining, I told myself. *You knew what his life was like when you got involved with him. Just be glad that he cut back on his projects after he moved here.*

That was true enough. When he was climbing his way to become the box-office star that he currently was, he'd done four and sometimes even five movies a year, shooting them back to back, never letting up. At least now he only took on three per year, meaning that he was here in Las Vegas more than half the time.

"Then it sounds like we have a plan," I said. "Breakfast, and then I'll throw you out so we can both get some work done."

He just smiled. "All right. But let me take you out to Smoky Joe's tonight."

That sounded like a perfect way to end the day. We'd be able to see each other again, and, if I'd had any luck with the tea leaves, I'd be able to tell him all about it.

"It's a deal," I said. "Now, though, let's eat."

Max left a little before eleven, and, as usual, the house felt way too empty without him there. But I told myself I had plenty to keep me occupied, and the laundry definitely wasn't going to wait.

After I got the first load going, though, my gaze fell on Mandy's portrait, which I'd left sitting on the mantel. I still felt just jangly enough that doing a reading didn't seem like a very good idea. It would need to wait until after lunch, which was generally when I liked to bust out the tea leaves, anyway. For whatever reason, I tended to have better luck in the afternoons.

And that meant I had at least a half hour to kill before I needed to shift the current load into the dryer. Because it was after ten but not lunchtime yet, it seemed the perfect window of opportunity to head over to Andrew Carson's house.

Unless, of course, he was at church, but I somehow doubted anyone who lived such a solitary existence would spend his Sunday mornings leaving the house and socializing with other human beings. No, he might be doing his own chores, but I could almost guarantee that he'd be there when I dropped by.

I took Mandy's photo from the mantel,

grabbed my purse on my way out the back door, and headed to the garage. Maybe I could have walked, since the Carson house really wasn't that far from mine, but it looked like it might try to rain, and I didn't want the portrait to get wet.

As was the case on most Sundays in my hometown, the streets of Las Vegas seemed quiet enough. Although I now knew Mr. Carson was friendly, I still didn't presume to pull into the driveway of his house, but instead parked at the curb just as I had the day before.

He answered the doorbell almost immediately, seeming to tell me he'd been waiting for me, even though I hadn't really told him exactly when I'd be over to return Mandy's portrait. Instead of saying hello, he asked, "Everything went all right?"

"It went perfectly," I told him as I stepped inside the house. "Mandy's *ofrenda* looked wonderful. I took pictures if you want to see how it was set up."

"No," he said at once, "that's all right. But I'm glad there weren't any problems."

"Then here you go," I said, and handed over the picture. He took it from me, murmured that he was going to put it back, and disappeared down the hallway that I assumed led to the bedrooms.

I stood there awkwardly in the entry, since I didn't know what else to do. Mr. Carson hadn't invited me to sit down like he had the last time I visited, so I just waited for him to return.

To my surprise, he was carrying a large book in one hand, a volume that turned out to be a Las Vegas High School yearbook from 1984, Mandy's sophomore year. He put it in my mystified hands, saying, "I thought maybe this would help you, provide some clues or something." A corner of his mouth lifted ever so slightly as he added, "I'm not sure how any of this works."

I almost told him I didn't, either, then decided it probably wasn't a good idea for the person who was trying to solve his daughter's murder to admit she really didn't know what she was doing.

"Thanks," I said. "It'll definitely help me learn a little more about Mandy's circle of friends, the people she knew."

"That's what I was hoping," he replied. A slight pause, and he went on, "I had to give you the one from her sophomore year because it's the last one that people signed. They had a big memorial page in her junior yearbook and gave me a copy, but no one wrote in it."

No, with Mandy dying in October, months and months before the yearbooks were handed out, there wouldn't have been any opportunity for her classmates to write all those slogans—"have a great summer!" "see you next year!"—that seemed to be standard fare when people didn't know what else to say.

"It's perfect," I said, and hoped I was right. There was every possibility that I wouldn't find anything of note, nothing that would tell me anything more than what I already knew. "And I'll be sure to let you know if I turn up something interesting."

Again, he surprised me, this time by giving a small shake of his head. "No, I don't want to know all the twists and turns. You tell me when you find the monster who really strangled my daughter in that damn park."

And then he looked toward the door, a clear dismissal. As far as I could tell, he wanted to help me, but not at the expense of the fragile peace of mind he'd managed to maintain over the last few decades.

Well, I would respect his wishes. After murmuring another thank-you, I let myself out and hurried down the front walk to the spot where my sky-blue Subaru was parked at the curb. I set the yearbook down on the passenger seat and headed for home.

I had a lot of work to do.

Although maybe it would have been smarter to do the tea-leaf reading first, I instead laid the yearbook down on the kitchen table, took a brief detour into the laundry room so I could shift things around, and then came back into the kitchen. A half-drunk glass of water sat on the counter, so I refreshed it before going over to the table and sitting down at one of the two chairs placed there.

Curious, I flipped back to the sophomore class so I could see Mandy's photo. It wasn't all that different from the one her father had let me borrow for her *ofrenda,* although her hair wasn't curled in this one, but lay sleek and pale against the dark top she was wearing. Those blonde locks also looked a little shorter in this picture, telling me she'd let it grow during the intervening year.

A page back was Evelyn Hodge's school portrait, although she was Evelyn Gardner here. She was almost unrecognizable, with her brown hair in a curly perm and braces on her teeth, although once I looked past those unfortunate details, I could see something of the graceful-looking woman she'd turned out to be.

Somewhere in between them was Jeff Hodge's picture. He'd been a good-looking boy, with thick brown hair and friendly brown eyes. I had no doubt that he and Mandy had made a pretty spectacular couple, just as Max and Raylene Bryant had when we were all in high school.

The similarities stopped there, though. Max and Raylene had split up after their senior year, when he'd decided to go to New Mexico University in Albuquerque, and even though Raylene would have been all too happy to get back together with him when he returned to Las Vegas, he'd made his feelings on that subject abundantly clear.

I twisted the diamond band on my ring finger, watching as the stones sparkled in the wan light that came through the kitchen window. Back then, I might have dreamed of being Max Sullivan's fiancée, but I'd never thought it would actually happen.

Which dreams of Mandy's had been cut short?

Well, I couldn't give her back the life that had been stolen from her, but I could make damn sure that the person responsible didn't spend another day walking free in the world.

As I flipped through the pages of the yearbook and read the notes—telling myself I wasn't snooping, that these messages had been left almost forty years ago and that Mandy's father had given me permission to look at them—I started to form a clearer picture of what her life had been back then. Yes, she'd obviously been popular...pretty much every blank space had been filled...but it also seemed as if her closest circle had consisted of Evelyn, someone named Julie Ingram, and two other girls, Susan Lopez and Cathy Engel.

None of those names seemed at all familiar to me, but I told myself that wasn't too strange. Odds were that Julie and Susan and Cathy had gotten married in the intervening years and changed their names, even if they'd stayed in Las Vegas—which wasn't a given, because people left all the time, moving to Santa Fe or Albuquerque or even farther away for school and better career opportunities.

Still....

One of my regulars was a woman named Cathy Newman, and she would be around the right age, in her early fifties somewhere. The next time she came in, I'd have to ask her whether she'd gone to high school with Mandy. Maybe she wouldn't have anything of any real import to tell me...but maybe she would.

I also noticed a long note on the page with a picture of the science club, a note from a boy named Scott Emerson. Even reading it now, years after it had been there, it made me want to cringe —way too complimentary, telling Mandy she was the nicest and prettiest girl in school, and that he really hoped they'd be able to hang out sometime this summer.

Because the note was on the same page as the science club photo, I could pick out Scott easily enough. He'd been one of those gangly guys who probably had shot up six inches in one year, half a head taller than the other boys in the club, all arms and legs and a prominent Adam's apple.

Even if Mandy hadn't been dating Jeff Hodge, I doubted she would have given Scott Emerson the time of day. That she'd let him sign her yearbook at all seemed a little strange, but then again, maybe not, considering it looked as though everyone in her entire class had written her some kind of note.

Had Scott been stalking Mandy, formed some kind of obsession about her? It didn't take too much imagination to see him getting frustrated by any rebuff on her part, to think he might have taken matters into his own hands...so to speak.

I told myself I was reading a whole heck of a lot into one awkward note in a yearbook. Thousands of guys had crushes on girls that were never reciprocated. It wasn't as if teenage frustration automatically resulted in murder.

But...what if it had?

I closed the yearbook and went upstairs to the bedroom I used as an office. My MacBook Air sat on the desk, its lid closed, since days sometimes went by without me opening it.

In this particular case, though, I thought it would be better to have the laptop's bigger screen rather than trying to do this on my phone.

It didn't take too long to get some results on my search for "Scott Emerson Las Vegas New Mexico." Not that he lived here anymore, though;

no, it looked as though he'd gone to college at UNM, had actually gotten a doctorate in physics there, and had stayed on to teach. He now appeared to live in Albuquerque, although the online search didn't say exactly where.

That was all right, though. I could probably talk Kyle into giving me the man's address, if it turned out I thought an in-person conversation was warranted. That might not have been exactly kosher—I knew deputies weren't supposed to use their access to special police databases to do favors for friends—but I had to believe Kyle wouldn't have a problem helping me solve a cold case that had been in the Las Vegas P.D.'s books since before either of us was even born.

On the surface, it definitely looked as though Scott had moved on from his high school crush. Or had he left his hometown, never to return, because he was smart enough to remove himself from the scene of the crime?

Again, I had no idea.

Still, I had a piece of information I hadn't possessed before, another person who might have had a reason to intercept Mandy Carson in the park that dark October night so many years ago. She didn't know who had strangled her, but it wasn't too hard to imagine tall, awkward Scott Emerson slipping out from behind a tree and throttling her with his long, clever fingers.

Okay, that was a bit of a stretch on my part, since I had no idea whether he'd had big hands. However, my own high school days weren't so far behind me that I couldn't remember some of the guys I'd had classes with, the way they seemed all out of proportion, as if some parts of them had grown faster than others.

I closed the laptop.

Time to see if the tea leaves had anything to tell me.

CHAPTER 10

Stalkarazzi

I headed down to the kitchen and put the kettle on to boil. Quite possibly, I wasn't feeling as serene and grounded as I should have been when attempting a tea-leaf reading, but I'd promised Max I would do this, and I still had some time before I had to take the current load out of the dryer.

Besides, I was curious to see what the leaves might tell me.

Because the kettle was only half full, it didn't take too long for it to boil. I placed the customary scoop of gunpowder green tea in the antique teacup I always used for these readings, then waited for it to cool enough so I could start sipping.

During this part of the proceedings, I knew I needed to let my mind grow calm, to allow myself to open up to whatever messages the leaves might want to send me. I also had to focus on the question I wanted answered, and to make it as clear as possible.

In this particular case, that wasn't too difficult.

Who killed Mandy Carson?

I sipped the tea, holding that question in my mind, until the tea was mostly gone. Then it was time to tip the cup over onto its saucer in order to get the last bits of liquid out of the teacup, and finally, turn it right-side up so I could get a clearer look at the shapes of the leaves left behind.

They'd mostly settled at the bottom, not telling me very much...but there was a definite blob in the center that looked almost exactly like a key. In tea-leaf readings, a key was generally a symbol of opportunities that needed to be unlocked, or possibly missed opportunities, if the tea leaves had clustered near the bottom of the cup.

How was Mandy Carson in a position to unlock opportunities when she'd been dead for almost forty years?

I released a breath and peered back into the cup, hoping I might have missed something, but it was pretty clear that the key-shaped clump of leaves on almost the equator of the surface was the only thing even approaching a defined shape.

Maybe the leaves were trying to tell me one particular clue was the key to unlocking the mystery of Mandy's death. If that was the case, though, they were going to have to work a lot harder to show exactly which clue was the center of the conundrum.

Just as I set the teacup down, the dryer buzzed inside the laundry room. That seemed to put a period to my reading, and I got up from my chair, rinsed out the cup, and went to retrieve my load of darks.

Either the answer would come to me...or it wouldn't.

No bursts of inspiration for the rest of that afternoon, nothing to tell me exactly where I needed to look next. I supposed I could have texted Kyle and asked him to look into Scott Emerson for me, but that kind of request seemed to be the sort of thing that was better made in person.

Instead, I finished the laundry, did some housework, and tried my best to stop obsessing over a puzzle that had way too many missing pieces. I just had to hope that when I talked it over with Max at dinner, he might have some insights he could offer me, a different angle of looking at the problem that would allow me to see my way clear to the right answer.

At the very least, I'd be able to spend the evening with him, and that was guaranteed to put me in a much better mood.

He showed up promptly at 6:30, as promised. I knew he had been working very hard lately to be more punctual, mostly because he'd realized that my work schedule didn't have a lot of wiggle room, and his former lackadaisical attitude toward his arrival times wouldn't earn him any brownie points.

A quick kiss after I answered the door, and then I locked up and followed him down the porch steps and along the front walk to his waiting Bronco. After we'd both buckled our seatbelts, he pulled away from the curb and headed toward downtown.

"I'm guessing that frown you're wearing means you didn't get anything useful from the tea leaves," he remarked.

Had I been frowning? I resisted the urge to reach up and touch my forehead to be sure.

"Not really," I said. "They showed me a key, which doesn't seem to have much to do with Mandy's particular situation. Her dad gave me one of her yearbooks, though."

"Oh?" Max replied, sending a quick glance in my direction before he looked back at the road ahead of us. "Anything interesting in there?"

"Maybe," I said. "There was one kind of geeky guy who seemed a little obsessive about her, but it's hard to gauge that sort of thing just by reading a note in a yearbook. All the same, I think I'm going to ask Kyle if he can look up where the guy is living now, in case I decide I need to talk to him."

"You don't have to bother Kyle," Max said at once. He turned onto Bridge Street, as usual finding a perfect parking place only a few yards down from Smoky Joe's, our destination. "Al can do it for you."

I blinked at Max as he expertly maneuvered the Bronco into the space he'd found. Obviously, all those stunt driving courses he'd taken had seriously upped his parallel-parking game. "He can?"

"Yep." Max shut off the engine, then turned toward me. "He has a P.I. license. Never uses it, but he still has access to all those databases. What's the guy's name?"

"Scott Emerson," I said. "He lives in Albuquerque and is a physics professor at UNM."

"Should be easy to find." Max got his phone out of his pocket and sent off a quick text—presumably to Al so he could do a little research while the two of us were noshing on smoked brisket. "He's working on it," he added after a moment. "With any luck, he'll have some information for us soon enough. Shall we?"

I nodded, and the two of us got out of the car. Although we'd arrived right smack in the middle of the dinner rush, I wasn't too worried about getting a table. After the *Fix My Town* team had bailed on Las Vegas midway through their shoot, Max had stepped in to finance the various projects that had been in progress, including the complete remodel of the old cowboy emporium that Smoky Joe's now occupied. The owners had been so grateful that they'd made sure Max would always have a prime table, no matter when he showed up.

Which proved to be the case today, because the hostess greeted us and immediately guided Max and me to a quiet table in the back. A couple of people waiting to be seated gave us the stink-eye, but since I didn't recognize them, I guessed they were probably tourists. Everyone in town knew about the arrangement Max had with the restaurant and didn't have a problem with it, mostly because, without him, the place wouldn't exist at all.

I was kind of surprised the people giving us dirty looks hadn't realized who he was, but maybe hunger trumped being star-struck.

Soon enough, a server named Naomi came and took our order, since by then we basically had the menu memorized and didn't need to waste time trying to figure out what we wanted to eat. A few minutes after that, she reappeared with the bottle of wine we'd ordered, opened it, and poured some for the two of us.

"Much better," I said after I took a sip. "This whole thing has me more stressed out than I thought it would."

"But wasn't disaster averted after you did Mandy's *ofrenda* for her yesterday?" Max asked, and then drank some of his own cabernet.

I grimaced. "Only temporarily. She's promised to keep causing havoc until we get this figured out. It's kind of like the Day of the Dead festival woke her up or something, and now she wants the mystery solved once and for all."

Max reached up to run a hand through his shaggy light brown hair. When he was between films, he tended to let it grow out, more because he claimed he didn't care for any of the local stylists than because he was trying to make a fashion statement. I'd offered to trim it once, mostly to see how he would react, and he'd just grinned and said he might take me up on that one day.

In the meantime, though, he always looked just a little disheveled...and therefore that much sexier.

"Well, I can't blame her for wanting some closure after all these years," he remarked. "Hanging around that park must get pretty old."

I couldn't really argue with that observation, so I just nodded and had some more wine. "Maybe if we can find out who the murderer is, Mandy will finally be at peace and will be able to move on."

At least, that was the hope I'd been holding close to my heart. I still couldn't claim to know exactly what conditions needed to be met before an earthbound spirit decided it was time to ascend to the next plane of existence—or however you wanted to phrase it—but it seemed to me that if she no longer had such a terrible secret hanging over her, she'd be able to find some measure of serenity.

"I think she will," Max said, sounding confident as only he could. "Especially with you on the case."

Too bad I didn't feel as sure of a happy outcome as he did. Even though I did my best to remind myself that I'd nabbed my share of criminals over the past year, that feat had been a lot easier to manage than this particular case, thanks to dealing with a murder that had just occurred. Trying to piece everything together so many years after the fact made the entire process a lot more difficult.

I didn't voice those fears, however, only said, "I hope so."

The food arrived then—a variety platter for Max and half a smoked chicken for me—and we ate in silence for a few minutes. Even after we picked up the conversation, we guided it to less fraught topics, like our upcoming wedding.

"Whatever date you think is best," he told me after he'd eaten a forkful of cheesy grits. "I won't need to leave again until the end of May, so we have some time to work with."

Even though I knew it was part of his job, I

couldn't help quailing a little at the thought of being left alone for more than a month so soon after our wedding. Luckily, though, he didn't seem to notice anything strained about my expression, so it was easy enough to reply, "I was thinking maybe the last Saturday in April. There's at least a fifty-fifty chance the weather will be decent."

Max grinned at my comment, as I'd hoped he would. "Those odds aren't too bad. Besides, I figured we'd rent the ballroom at the Plaza. It's really the only place in town that's big enough, and with an indoor event, we won't have to worry about the weather so much."

Because I'd also been thinking the Ilfeld Ballroom was the perfect venue for the reception, his comment didn't come as too much of a surprise. "Oh, you're expecting a big crowd?" I asked, my tone arch.

His smile didn't waver for a second. Instead, he put down his fork so he could reach over and run a caressing finger across the back of my hand. Just that light touch was enough to send a pleasant shiver through me, although I did my best not to react too much.

"Skye, you know the whole town is going to want to be there."

Probably, although even the hotel's ballroom wasn't big enough to accommodate such a crowd. But we'd have Max's mom and dad, extended family, friends of his from L.A., the wedding party, and all my own friends here in Las Vegas. I didn't know whether my cousins in Texas would want to come all that way when they never made any special effort to visit me, and then wanted to laugh at myself. Maybe they would have stayed home for an ordinary wedding, but I doubted they'd want to miss seeing their cousin marry a genuine Hollywood box office phenomenon.

"I think we might have to limit the guest list just a little," I joked, and his bright blue eyes glinted with amusement.

"Probably." His phone pinged then, and although we both had a fairly strict no-devices policy during dinner, he went ahead and pulled it out. "Al dug up some information on your physics professor. I'll send it to you."

"Thanks," I replied, thinking that had been pretty fast. On the other hand, Scott Emerson worked at a local university. It wasn't as if he'd been keeping a particularly low profile.

Speaking of low profiles....

"Or we could just elope," I said casually, and Max practically choked on the sip of cabernet he'd been about to swallow.

"You don't seriously mean that, do you?"

No, I didn't. Not exactly, anyway, but....

"You know someone's going to leak our wedding plans to the press," I said. "So maybe it would be smarter to just disappear and do the deed."

The smile he'd been wearing vanished immediately. "I'm not going to let those jackals keep us from having the wedding I know you want. We'll just have to hire extra security."

I didn't much like the idea of having a bunch of rent-a-cops hanging around our ceremony and the reception that followed. On the other hand, I liked even less the thought of sneaking off to get married. Call me a traditionalist, but I wanted the whole deal—the dress and the flowers and the cake, and our friends and family looking on.

"Okay," I said, and even managed to smile a little. "I'm sure Lou and Al will be more than happy to arrange our own private army."

"Damn straight."

We picked up our wine glasses and clinked them against each other to seal the deal, and finished our food. Max handed over his black Amex card when Naomi came to check on us— he'd had to be firm with Smoky Joe's owners, and had told them in no uncertain terms that while he was okay with always getting seated no matter how busy the place was, he wasn't going to let them comp his meals—and the two of us stood up soon after he got his card back, then pulled on our jackets and headed out of the restaurant...

...only to be hit by the glare of what felt like a

thousand flashes going off at once. Okay, after I blinked to clear my vision, I realized there were only about ten or so paparazzi lying in wait for us, but that was ten too many.

Max, who was an old pro at this, didn't even break stride, but tightened his grip on my hand and pushed his way through the crowd, ignoring their questions about our engagement, and whether he wanted to make a statement. Clearly, he didn't, because he stayed tight-lipped and grim as we hurried over to the Bronco and got inside.

For a moment or two, I feared they were going to block our way, to trap us at the curb so they could keep snapping pictures. To my infinite relief, however, they stepped back as we pulled away and accelerated down Bridge Street, and a minute later, they weren't anything but a bad memory.

"Sorry about that," Max said in clipped tones that didn't sound very much like him.

"It's okay," I replied, even as I wondered why he was apologizing. "None of it was your fault."

"Maybe not directly," he said, maneuvering down a side street, and then another. This wasn't the way home, but I thought I knew what he was doing. I hadn't noticed anyone following us, and yet I guessed he was trying his best to hide our trail, to make it hard to figure out where we were going. "But still, I knew that once I put that ring on your finger, someone would start talking about it, and soon enough, the stalkers would descend."

"They've left you alone all these months," I pointed out, but he only shrugged.

"That's because I haven't done anything news-worthy," he responded. "But Max Sullivan getting engaged is a big deal to them."

I leaned over and placed a quick kiss on his cheek. "It's a big deal to me, too."

He smiled...a little. "I know, sweetheart. I just wish you didn't have to deal with any of this."

Well, I wished I didn't, either. But the paparazzi were a small price to pay compared to having Max in my life, so I'd do my best to shrug it off. "It's okay. At least I kind of know what it's like, since these jerks were hanging around when you were accused of Perry's murder, too."

Max's lips thinned ever so slightly. Even though he'd been completely exonerated, I still knew he didn't like to think about those awful days when the entire world had thought he'd killed the director of *Perdition Road* in a fit of pique.

"That went away quickly, though," he said. "This...this could last a lot longer. Are you ready to deal with that?"

"If I have to," I said stoutly. I'd put up with a lot more than a couple of jackasses with cameras in order to be with Max Sullivan.

He took one hand off the wheel, and reached

over so he could twine his fingers with mine and give them a gentle squeeze. "You're amazing," he told me, then went on as he released my hand, "But we might need to talk about you coming to stay at my place."

I stared at him, startled. "Why?"

"Because I have security, and you don't. No one can get past the fences on my property without either Al or Lou knowing about it and handling the situation, but your house doesn't have anything like that. Any of those bastards could walk right up to your front door, or be lurking in the bushes when you leave for work. Do you really want to deal with that for the next six months?"

No, I didn't...especially since I'd had my own run-ins with a paparazzo who'd thought it was a good idea to stake out my house and my coffee shop back when Max was accused of murder. And speaking of the shop....

"Even if I come stay with you," I said slowly, "that won't keep them away from Levitation Latte."

"No," Max replied without missing a beat. "But I'll hire someone else to keep an eye on your store if I have to. We can work that part out."

"Then why not hire a security guard to watch my house?" I persisted.

For a second, he didn't reply. "You don't want to stay with me?" he asked, voice a little too flat.

Yikes. I'd known we would have to have this conversation sooner or later, but I really hadn't thought it would happen because we'd just gotten chased away from Smoky Joe's by a bunch of camera-wielding goons.

"That's not what I said," I replied, speaking slowly because I knew I had to choose my words with care. "I mean, I always knew we would end up at your ranch—it's bigger and more private...and, like you said, has a lot more security. But I love my house, and I guess I just didn't think I'd have to leave it behind so soon."

Another of those pauses, although something felt different about this one. When he spoke, his tone was very gentle.

"I get it," he said. "You grew up in that house. Your grandmother left it to you. That's why I didn't pressure you to move in with me before now. But...."

The words trailed off, and he gave a small hitch of his shoulders, one that seemed strangely vulnerable.

"But now things have changed," I finished for him. Because he'd just turned down onto my street, I didn't try to take his fingers again, and only laid my hand on his leg. "I get it."

And I did. I supposed Max and I had both been fooling ourselves if we hadn't thought the paparazzi would turn up just as soon as word of our engagement got leaked. Maybe after a few days or weeks, they'd get bored and move on...or maybe they'd keep hanging around, waiting until the actual wedding itself so they could get some real money shots.

"Still," I went on, and hesitated. The request might sound strange to him, but I knew I needed my own chance to say goodbye to the house that was the only home I'd ever known. "I want to stay here tonight. Just this one last night. You can send Lou or Al over to keep an eye on me if it'll make you feel better. Then tomorrow after work, I'll pack a bunch of my things and come stay at the ranch."

Not all of my stuff, of course, but the clothes and toiletries I'd need for a week's stay, and some items from the kitchen that I knew Max didn't have at his place but which were necessary for me to get by while cooking. As for exactly what I would do about my house itself, I had no idea.

Well, it was paid for. It wasn't as if I'd be carrying a mortgage on a home I wasn't even occupying.

Max pulled into my driveway but kept the engine running. "I understand," he said quietly. "You need to say goodbye to the house. But I'm sending Al over, and I'll come help you pack tomorrow after work."

And this...this was exactly why I loved him so

much. No arguments, no protests that it was silly to feel so attached to four walls and a roof. He'd known me pretty much my entire life, and that meant he knew what was important to me.

"I love you," I told him, and he smiled.

"I know."

CHAPTER 11

Trading Places

As weird as it felt to know that Al was standing guard as I got ready for bed, I had to admit Max's concern had been warranted. Only about ten minutes after he dropped me off, a bunch of cars came down my block, driving way too fast, jockeying for position for the prime spot across the street from the house. Luckily, I was already inside by then with all the doors and windows locked, but still.

However, Al showed up just a few minutes later, pulling his white SUV into my driveway. I didn't know for sure whether or not any of the paparazzi would have been bold enough to park there, but with Al's 4Runner now occupying that spot, I didn't have to worry about them encroaching on my property.

I did feel guilty about him having to stay up all night to keep watch on the house, even though I tried to tell myself that he would have been doing the same thing at Max's place. That's how they managed it, with the two bodyguards taking turns on duty to ensure constant coverage. And while I didn't like the idea of only Lou being there to guard the ranch, I knew the entire property was fenced and protected by security cameras, and therefore much more defensible than my own home.

As best I could, I got ready for bed without trying to think about those cars parked on my street, vehicles occupied by men who didn't seem to think there was anything materially wrong about invading other people's lives just so they could get a few shots for the tabloids. Even with Al's vigilance, I couldn't shake off the uneasiness, similar to the feeling I had when there was a bee in the house that I couldn't locate, anxiously anticipating a sudden sting.

I turned off the light, making sure that all those lurking paparazzi would have a hard time figuring out precisely when I'd gone to bed. Even so, I lay there for a long moment, wanting to absorb every creak, every whisper of air from the furnace, every familiar sound that had been a part of my life for as long as I could remember.

After tonight, I might very well never sleep here again.

And that was okay. I'd be sharing Max's home, and then it would become our home, and soon enough, we would have a hard time remembering that we'd ever lived apart.

Or at least, I hoped that was how things were going to shake out. I'd stayed over at his house before, but only after we thought someone had broken in and stolen Calum McRae's laptop. That time, I'd slept in the guest bedroom, because I hadn't wanted to rouse Max when I had to get up at four-thirty so Levitation Latte would be ready for its usual opening time of seven o'clock.

Well, he'd have to get used to my schedule, one way or another. He'd claimed to be one of those people who could fall asleep almost anywhere or anytime, citing years of dealing with early call times on set and generally unpredictable shooting schedules.

Soon enough, we'd be putting that claim to the test.

I rolled over on my side and wondered whether I should stay away from work tomorrow. It wasn't so late that I couldn't text Deanne and let her know what was going on, and say that I thought it might be a good idea to keep Levitation Latte closed for another day in the hope that maybe the paparazzi would get bored and move on to other, less elusive targets.

Somehow, though, I knew they wouldn't give up that easily. Besides, I didn't want to act like such a coward. Was I really going to let them chase me away from the business I'd worked so hard to make a success?

Well, you're letting them chase you away from your house, I thought sourly.

That wasn't completely true, though. I'd always known—well, at least since things had gotten serious between us—that I'd end up moving in with Max eventually. The celebrity-hungry photographers had only sped up the process.

All right, I'd go to work tomorrow. Max had already said that he'd get a security guard for my store if necessary, so I really didn't have any valid reason for not opening at seven o'clock that Monday morning as usual.

And I'd had a crazy couple of days and needed to sleep.

I shut my eyes, and willed myself to slumber.

It didn't feel exactly like a dream. I'd seen this glade before—it was the one I'd created in my mind during the séance we'd held at Max's house a year ago, the same spot where I'd met with Ana

Moreno's spirit and learned the terrible secret she'd been hiding.

That wasn't Ana approaching me, however.

No, it was my grandmother Maureen.

She'd met me here that first time, more than a year ago, when I'd been trying to communicate with Tom Gallegos' ghost. Back then, she'd told me I shouldn't be meddling in the world of the spirits, that my talents didn't lie in that direction. More than once since then, I'd guiltily wondered what she would think if she'd seen me talking with the various ghosts I'd encountered along the way.

Had she appeared now to read me the riot act and tell me I needed to walk away from Mandy Carson's cold case?

I truly hoped not, because I'd promised Mandy I would do my best to find the truth...and I wasn't the kind of person who walked away from her promises.

As before, my grandmother appeared looking like herself in the prime of life, maybe in her late thirties, hair still untouched by gray and blue eyes cheerful and bright. I really didn't look anything like her, but at least I'd inherited her skills in the kitchen.

"Hi, Grandma," I said, hoping I sounded natural, and not as though I'd been wracking my brains trying to figure out why she would be meeting me here.

"Hello, Skye," she replied. Her expression seemed cheerful enough, which I hoped was a good omen. "I thought I should talk to you."

"In my dream?"

Her mouth quirked a little. "This isn't exactly a dream. It's more like...a meeting place on another plane."

Fair enough. Although I'd traveled here before, I definitely didn't understand the mechanics of how all this worked. For me, it was good enough just to know that I could come to this place when necessary.

"So...what did you want to talk to me about?" I asked, steeling myself for the inevitable dressing-down.

To my surprise, she said, "I wanted to apologize to you."

"'Apologize'?" I repeated, still not sure what was going on. True, my grandmother had never been the sort of person to hold a grudge, or to hold back an apology when one was warranted, but still, that wasn't what I'd been expecting to hear.

Mouth still curved in a smile, she said, "When I met you here that last time, I told you the world of the spirits wasn't something you should be meddling with. But the events of the past year have proved me very wrong."

"Then...why did you say it?" I asked. Honestly, I wasn't even annoyed...just mystified.

Her expression sobered. "Because I was worried that my mother's talents and your mother's magic wouldn't mix, that you could get in over your head before you realized it. Not all spirits on the other planes are benign, you know. There was a chance— a large one, I thought—that you might call something to you that you couldn't control."

Well, that was reassuring...not. Because as disconcerting as it had been to talk to spirits like Mandy's or even Ana's, I'd known they had once been regular people, and were only looking for some kind of closure, some measure of peace. The thought that I might have made contact with something that meant me harm—or harm to the people I cared about—made me cold all over.

"That's not what happened, though," my grandmother continued. "You've done good work with the spirits you've met, and what you're trying to do for poor Miss Carson is admirable as well. In your work with ghosts, it seems as if you've tapped into the O'Malley magic only, and nothing from the Petrucci side of the family."

I supposed that made some sense. After all, Alicia herself had told me that her family's magic was all about affecting the physical world, and had nothing to do with the world of the spirits. And unnerving as it sometimes was to communicate with ghosts, I'd much rather do that than work with the Petrucci magic, which seemed frighteningly powerful and something that could get out of control very easily.

"And that's good, right?" I said.

My grandmother smiled. "Yes, it's good. My mother received messages from those who'd passed over, and those who remained caught on your plane. She also read tea leaves, like you do. It's obvious to me now that her gifts are very strong in you."

Honestly, I didn't know how strong they were, but considering I'd done things over the past year that I would never have imagined before that, it did seem as if something of my great-grandmother's talents had been passed on to me.

But....

"Why didn't you tell me all this about my great-grandmother?" I asked then. "I mean, you said a few things, but you never went into any detail."

My grandmother Maureen played with a fold of the white dress she was wearing, a full-skirted frock that looked like something straight out of a 1950s sitcom...or maybe *WandaVision*. "Because at the time, I wasn't sure how much of those talents you'd really inherited. You had true dreams sometimes, and you were good with tea leaves, but I'd never seen any sign of you communicating with spirits."

That was true enough. Smiling, I said, "Maybe

I just never had the opportunity. After all, our house isn't haunted."

She still looked serious, though, and said, "No, but plenty of other places in Las Vegas are. You never seemed particularly sensitive about the ghosts in the Plaza Hotel, or other places where they've been documented around town."

Again, I couldn't really contradict what she'd just said, because it was the truth. Sure, I'd gotten vaguely creeped out when going down to the restrooms on the lower level of the hotel, but it wasn't as if I'd seen any ghosts or even known for sure whether there was really something there or whether I was just doing a good job of scaring myself.

"Well, I always was a late bloomer," I said, hoping she would smile at the joke.

This time, the corners of her mouth lifted a little. "You were. So maybe it shouldn't be so surprising that this part of your talents came to you a bit later in life. Anyway, that's why I wanted to see you. I could tell you were feeling guilty about doing something I'd tried to warn you away from, and I wanted to let you know that you should continue to do this work if that's what you're called to do."

Was I "called"? It seemed like these past couple of times, I'd sort of stumbled into working with ghosts. I certainly hadn't sought them out on my own.

For all I knew, though, that was how the universe worked. You ended up exactly where you were supposed to be, even if you took a round-about way of getting there.

"I'm just trying to help Mandy," I said simply. "If I ever get this figured out, I'll be happy to never talk to a ghost again." I paused there as a thought popped into my mind. "I don't suppose you could tell me who murdered her?"

As I'd halfway expected, my grandmother shook her head. "I don't know who it was," she said sadly. "I remember when it happened, of course, but since I was alive at the time, I don't have access to any knowledge I wouldn't have otherwise had back then."

Interesting. Did that mean people on this other plane...whatever it was...knew much more about current events than they might have when they were still among the living?

I must have been wearing a perplexed expression, because she said, "Think of it a little like only being able to read what's on your bookshelf, then suddenly having access to the entire internet. It's a bit like that. But it's not as though we can see the thoughts of people we don't know, or anything close to that. Otherwise, I might have been able to look into the mind of Mandy's killer and see the guilt they've been hiding all these years."

"If the murderer was dead, would you know?"

"Probably not," my grandmother replied. She still wore that sad expression, as if she was recalling the nightmare of Mandy's death and the shock and horror that had swept through the town at the time. "But I have a feeling he's still there somewhere, thinking that he got away with it."

Not for much longer, I thought. *Not if I have anything to do about it.*

"Anyway," she went on, "I can't stay here for too long. I just wanted you to know that you're on the right path." She came closer and took me by the hand. Her fingers felt as real as mine, warm and comforting, just like they had when she was alive. A twinkle entered her blue-gray eyes, and she added, "And congratulations. I somehow knew you and Max would be together one day."

I blinked at her, startled, and then she let go of my hand and faded away. For a moment, I stood there in the glade, staring down at the shimmering band of diamonds on my left hand. More than anything, I wished my grandmother would have been able to attend the wedding, to watch Max and I become one, but this was all right, too.

She would be there in spirit, and had given us her blessing.

That was enough.

When I woke up the next morning, I felt more refreshed and full of energy than I'd been in a long time. Was that a byproduct of my meeting with my grandmother on that other plane, or was it simply the relief of knowing that she wasn't upset with me for continuing to communicate with ghosts despite her warning?

I didn't know, but that was okay. Either way, I had one less thing to worry about.

Not that I didn't have plenty more. A peek out my front window told me all those paparazzi were still parked on the street...and Al was still sitting in his 4Runner in the driveway, although it was hard to tell from that angle whether he was awake or just using his mere presence to keep the bloodhounds at bay.

When I checked my phone, I saw a text from Max had come through late the night before, long after I'd gone to sleep.

Al wants to drive you to work. We both think that will be safer. And the same security firm they used to work for is sending another guy to watch the shop. He should be there a little before seven.

Clearly, Max had been busy last night. And although I really didn't like the idea of getting chauffeured around town when I had a perfectly decent car waiting in my garage, I understood. The last thing I wanted was those goons chasing me, maybe causing a car accident. With any luck, the two of us would prove so elusive that the paparazzi would eventually give up and go back to whatever hole they crawled out of in the first place.

So I went ahead and did my usual morning prep, and slipped out the back door and locked it when I was done. When I approached the 4Runner and peeked inside, Al was awake and reaching over to unlock the doors.

"Thanks for this," I said as I slid inside. "I'm really sorry you had to sleep in my driveway all night."

He touched the ignition button, and the engine came to life. "It's fine," he replied with a grin. Like Lou, he was in his late fifties, stocky, with the kind of build that made it look as though he could put an entire platoon of paparazzi through a wall without even breaking a sweat. "I've slept in worse places."

I wanted to ask where, but figured that might be a little intrusive. Instead, I returned his grin, and settled against the seat as he put the SUV in reverse and began to back out of the driveway. Almost instantaneously, the lights of the various cars parked in front of my house turned on, but they seemed content to wait until we were moving forward to fall in behind us.

"Looks like we've got an escort," I remarked.

"Yeah," Al said. "No biggie. I was expecting them to do that. But they'll keep their distance."

Which they did, staying back a few car lengths as he made his way downtown and to my coffee shop. This didn't surprise me too much; the streets of Las Vegas weren't all that busy at the best of times, and now, at a little before five-thirty in the morning, they were practically deserted. I had no doubt the paparazzi would have been able to follow us, even if they'd been a quarter-mile back.

It wasn't like they didn't know where I was going.

When he pulled into the alley behind the shop, however, Al did so at an angle, creating an effective blockade. "When I unlock the door, you run for it," he told me. "They won't be able to get past me, and it'll take time for them to circle the block. You think you can get inside in time?"

"Sure," I said. It was only about ten yards to the back door of the shop, and I'd been a pretty good sprinter back in high school.

He shot me another grin, then touched the button to unlock the 4Runner's doors. I already had my purse slung over one shoulder, so it was easy enough for me to bolt out of the SUV and run like hell for the back door. Behind me, I heard tires squealing, telling me the paparazzi weren't about to challenge Al's impromptu blockade and instead were going to try heading me off at the pass.

Well, that wasn't going to happen.

I took the back steps two at a time, the key already in my hand. Just a few seconds to unlock the back door and slam it shut behind me, and a couple more to disengage the alarm. For a moment, I contemplated turning it back on, but that would only cause problems when Deanne showed up.

Yikes. I really needed to text her and let her know what was going on. Although it helped to have her here to get ready for opening, I could handle that on my own. Better for her to stay away until reinforcements arrived.

I got out my phone and sent her a quick message letting her know paparazzi were camped on the coffee shop's doorstep, and that she shouldn't come in until after seven when the security guard Max had hired arrived. In general, I would never have texted her that early, even if I knew she was probably already awake and getting ready for work, but this was an emergency.

Sure enough, her answer came back right away.

OMG. That's crazy! Will be there @ 7:10. Hang on!

See you then. And yeah, it's nuts.

To be honest, the hard part was already behind me. Now I was safely locked inside Levitation Latte, and now all I had to do was get ready for the day...and hope that Max's security guard was on time.

I got busy mixing batter, and, once the blue-berry and walnut spice muffins were in the oven, headed out front to get things ready for opening, now only forty-five minutes away. Luckily, the coffee shop had shades that I pulled down at the end of each day, so even if there were a bunch of paparazzi camped outside—and I had to believe there were—they wouldn't be able to see what I was doing or have a chance to take any pictures.

Just as I was heading back into the kitchen to check on the muffins, the cat door banged, and Tilly entered the room, looking even more annoyed than usual.

"Who in the world are all those people loitering in the alley?"

Obviously, the photographers weren't planning to decamp any time soon. "They're celebrity photographers," I explained.

Tilly's tail twitched. "I wasn't aware you were a celebrity."

"I'm not," I said serenely. By that point, I'd gotten used to the talking cat's somewhat jaun-diced view of the world, so her ironic tone didn't faze me. "But I just got engaged to one, and I guess some people think that's newsworthy."

That comment earned me a sniff, and Tilly headed over to the food and water bowls I refilled every morning. A dry, "Some people need to get a hobby," and then she buried her face in that morning's Salmon Surprise.

No kidding. But since I doubted the paparazzi lurking outside were going to suddenly abandon their posts because they'd gotten a wild hair to try knitting, I'd just have to go on with my day as best I could.

At around ten minutes 'til seven, I got a text. I pulled my phone out of my apron pocket, thinking maybe Deanne had decided to shoot me another message, but instead it was from a number I'd never seen before.

I'm at the front door. Max sent me.

Thank God.

All the same, I wasn't about to throw caution to the wind. I went up to the front window, pulled the blind aside ever so slightly, and saw a tall man in a black leather jacket and jeans—and with shoulders that looked as though they might not fit through the door—standing outside. A few yards past him stood a couple of other men with large cameras slung over their shoulders, both of them eyeing the newcomer with the kind of wariness usually reserved for a pair of gazelle who'd just seen a lion approach.

I got out my keys and unlocked the front door. One of the paparazzi looked as though he was about to take a step forward, but a single steely-eyed stare from the stranger kept him from moving.

So quickly that I almost couldn't see how he did it, the man slipped through the entrance and into the shop. I closed the door behind him and said, "Max sent you?"

"Yes, ma'am," the guy said. He looked like he was probably ten or fifteen years older than I was, so I didn't think the "ma'am" was warranted. However, judging by the way he looked and spoke, I had to believe he was former law enforcement, and probably addressed any woman over the age of eighteen the same way. "I'm Gordon Shaw."

"Hi, Gordon," I replied. "I'm Skye O'Malley. Thanks so much for watching the shop."

"That's what Mr. Sullivan hired me to do."

Clearly, Gordon Shaw was a no-nonsense kind of guy. And that was fine—he was here to keep the paparazzi away from me, not waste time with chitchat.

All the same, I thought I might as well be polite. "Would you like some coffee before you go back out? There's French roast and mocha java."

Maybe the taut set of his mouth relaxed ever so slightly. "Mocha java would be good."

I fixed him a go-cup, and told him where the cream and sugar and cinnamon were located. He gave the smallest shake of his head—obviously, Mr. Shaw was a no-frills coffee drinker, no big surprise

—and, cup in hand, he went back outside to take up his position near the door. No, he wasn't blocking it, but I could tell he was ready to lunge if anyone gave him the slightest trouble.

Shaking my head, I went back to the kitchen to get the muffins I'd just pulled out of the oven.

Somehow, I had a feeling this was going to be a very long day.

CHAPTER 12

Physical Attraction

Deanne came in at ten minutes after seven, just as promised. Eyes wide, she looked over one shoulder toward the door and said, "That's the guy Max hired?"

"Yes," I replied. "Gordon Shaw. Kind of impressive, isn't he?"

"That's one word for it," she said. "I just hope he doesn't scare off all the customers."

Her concerns proved to be valid, since we were much less busy that Monday morning than we usually would have been. I allowed myself a mental sigh and could only hope this situation wasn't permanent, that soon enough the paparazzi would realize they weren't getting anywhere near Max Sullivan's fiancée and would head for greener pastures.

At least, that was my hope. I could handle a couple of bad days, but if this kept up....

Deep down, I knew that even if Levitation Latte started losing money hand over fist, Max would step in to buoy me up. But I didn't want him to do that. There was no way I could ever level the playing field between us when it came to finances, and yet I wanted him to know I could make it on my own just fine without his help.

Whether I'd actually be able to stick to those lofty ideals was up to fate.

Lucy Margolis came in around ten-thirty, looking flustered. "Who is that man standing by the door?" she asked in a whisper, even though Gordon was outside and wouldn't have been able to hear anything she was saying. If it turned out he was going to be with me indefinitely, then he'd need to move his post inside when the weather turned really cold, but for now, he seemed content to keep watch from the sidewalk.

"A security guard," I said, hoping I didn't sound as tired as I felt. "We had to hire him to keep the paparazzi away from the store."

"The people standing across the street?"

I honestly hadn't realized Gordon had shooed the photographers all the way to the other side of Bridge Street, but that was probably because I'd been doing my best to stay away from the front door and windows. No, I'd been spending the far too wide gaps between customers by filling Deanne in on what had happened the night before, and how it looked as though I was going to be moving in with Max a lot sooner than I'd expected.

She'd been sympathetic, of course, and asked me what I planned to do with the house. Since I hadn't thought that far into the future, I'd only told her I'd worry about that later.

"Yes, I guess the word got out that I was engaged to Max," I told Lucy. "So they all showed up, hoping to get some shots of me. Luckily, he knew exactly what to do, and that's why we have Gordon here for the foreseeable future."

An expression of something that looked suspiciously like guilt flitted across Lucy's pleasant features. "Oh, no," she said, and I tilted my head at her.

"What's the matter?"

"I told Beth about your engagement when I was talking to her yesterday," she replied.

Beth was Lucy's younger sister, who'd moved to Albuquerque years ago. The two of them had remained close, though, with Lucy calling Beth at least a couple of times a week to keep her up to date on everything that was happening in her hometown.

"And she must have told someone else," Lucy went on. "This is all my fault."

Although I wanted to smile, I could tell she was

genuinely distressed. "No, it's not," I assured her. "This isn't the kind of news we could keep bottled up forever. Max probably knew it was only a matter of time before the story leaked and the paparazzi showed up. After all, it's not as though I've been trying to hide this."

And I lifted my left hand so the diamonds on my ring finger glittered in the illumination from the ceiling fixtures overhead.

"Still...." she said, obviously not wanting to let it go.

"Really, it isn't your fault," I said. "And this is only temporary. Eventually, they'll get bored and find someone else to harass."

Preferably very, very soon, although I knew I couldn't count on that.

Deanne came over with one of the walnut spice muffins Lucy loved so much already stowed in a bag, and a cup of mocha java in her other hand.

"Everything's fine," she told the older woman. "Skye's got me for backup."

A wavery little smile touched Lucy's lips, but it appeared she was ready to move on to other subjects, because she said, "Thank you for getting those for me. How much do I owe you?"

A question for form's sake only, since Lucy had been buying that combination for years and knew exactly what it cost.

However, Deanne didn't comment, only said, "Five eighty-nine."

Lucy handed over a ten-dollar bill and waited while Deanne made change. A moment later, she deposited several ones in the tip jar on the counter, said thank-you again, and headed out the door.

Once it had closed behind her, Deanne sent me a significant glance. "Do you really think she's responsible for the story leaking?"

"Of course not," I said tiredly. All the vim and vigor I'd woken up with that morning was gone, and now I only wanted the day to be over as quickly as possible. "Anyone could have done it—someone at Smoky Joe's, any of our customers from the past couple of days. If we'd really wanted to hide what was going on, we would have agreed that I should never wear the ring out in public."

"Right," she said. An awkward little silence, and then she added, "Are you okay? You just seem... weighed down."

A perfect description. I should have still been riding the high from Max proposing to me, but between trying to figure out what had really happened the night Mandy Carson was murdered and dodging paparazzi, I felt as though the entire weight of the world had descended on my shoulders.

And that didn't even take into account all the logistics that moving to Max's ranch was going to require. No wonder I just wanted to crawl into bed and sleep until all this was over.

Unfortunately, I wouldn't be allowed that escape. I summoned a smile that I guessed didn't fool Deanne for a single second, and said, "I'm fine. But let's brew up another batch of mocha java—Lucy's cup took most of what we had left in the pot."

Being Deanne, my friend didn't argue, or try to ask me any other questions. No, she just got out the bag of beans so I could grind some more, and stayed silent while I got the filtered water and poured it into the Breville coffeemaker.

As I made the coffee, I couldn't quite escape an overwhelming sense of futility. Okay, we needed this second batch, but by this time of the morning, we were usually on our third or fourth pot.

Yes, it was going to be a very long day.

Around one-thirty, Max texted me.

Gordon says it's slow. How're you holding up?

I wasn't sure how Gordon could gauge if we were having a slow day, since he'd never been to Levitation Latte before today. Not that it was worth mentioning.

I'm okay. Just wanting this day to be over.

Well, I have an idea. Since it's so slow, how about

I come pick you up and we take a drive down to Albuquerque?

While getting out of town sounded like a great idea, I wasn't sure why Max had suddenly gotten the notion to head south.

What's in Albuquerque?

Scott Emerson. His last class is over at 3. We can go talk to him and see what he can tell us about Mandy Carson.

I blinked. While I hadn't lost the thread of Mandy's murder investigation, I also had to admit I was feeling kind of flummoxed by the whole thing. I had my doubts whether Scott Emerson could tell us anything useful...but on the other hand, it probably wouldn't be very smart to discount him, either.

And I wouldn't bother to ask Max how he knew what Dr. Emerson's teaching schedule was. Al could have probably gotten his hands on that information even without the special access his private detective license allowed him.

Okay. Let me check with Deanne to see if it's okay if I bail.

I looked over at my friend, who was currently wiping down one table in a desultory sort of way, obviously trying to find whatever way she could to pass the time.

"Max wants to go with me to Albuquerque to talk to someone about Mandy's case," I said. "Do you think you can watch the shop on your own for the rest of the afternoon?"

At once, she straightened, expression brightening. "Do you have a new clue?"

"I'm not sure," I said. "But it's worth following up on."

A glance around the empty coffee shop, and she grinned. "I think I can manage here on my own for a couple of hours."

I'd been pretty sure that was how she was going to respond, but I returned her smile, anyway. "Thanks, Deanne—you're the best."

"Oh, I know," she replied, still smiling.

I went back to my phone.

We're good to go. But how're you going to evade the paps?

I'll come pick you up at the back door in the alley. Just be ready to run.

Got it.

Be there in 10.

I sent him a thumbs-up emoji, then returned the phone to my pocket. There weren't any windows in the back of the shop, so I wouldn't be able to check the alley to see if some paparazzi were lurking there as well. About all I could do was hope that they'd figured if the public part of Levitation Latte was this boring, then the rear entrance must be even worse. After letting Deanne know I would be leaving soon, I went into the back, put my phone in my purse, and took off my apron.

Should I let Gordon know I was bailing?

Probably, but I really didn't want to stick my head out the front door and alert the paparazzi that something was up.

Once again, Deanne came to my rescue in my time of need. I explained my predicament, and she said, "No problem. I'll let him know you're sneaking out the back."

"You're the best," I told her, and she shrugged.

"Well, top five at least."

I chuckled, then went into the back room and waited by the door. Sure enough, a text popped up on my phone just a moment later.

Coming around the corner now.

Time to go. I made sure my purse was slung firmly over one shoulder, then unlocked the back door and hurried out. Max's black Bronco slowed to a barely noticeable roll, and I opened the passenger door and jumped in.

Not a moment too soon—from the corner of one eye, I glimpsed a couple of men hurrying down the alley, cameras already raised.

They were too late, though. Max's foot hit the gas as I was buckling my seatbelt, and we bolted down the alley at way more than the posted fifteen miles per hour. A moment later, we were turning onto Bridge Street a block away from the spot where most of the paparazzi had been lurking, and I knew we'd gotten away clean.

"Pretty slick," Max commented, then paused at a red light before making right onto Grand Avenue, heading for the highway. "That felt like reenacting a scene from one of my movies."

"Except usually you're running from Russian agents or whatever," I joked, and he grinned.

"There are a lot of days when I'd rather be dealing with the Russians than a bunch of paparazzi."

He had a point there. Those people were as persistent as a dog with a bone.

I settled against the back of the seat, glad that we'd been able to escape, and extra glad that we'd be spending the rest of the afternoon far away from Las Vegas and our mob of stalkers. True, I would have liked the chance to go home and change out of my black long-sleeved T-shirt and jeans into something a little better suited for meeting with a physics professor, but we'd already been pressing our luck by having Max come to pick me up at the shop. There was no way we could have gone by my house and still managed to successfully evade pursuit. For all I knew, there were still some photographers staked out at my place, hoping to catch a glimpse of me as I returned home from work.

"So, what's our strategy for meeting with Scott

Emerson?" I asked, figuring I might as well change the subject to something a little more pleasant. "I mean, I assume we're not going to just walk in there and ask him if he murdered Mandy Carson thirty-eight years ago."

A corner of Max's mouth lifted. "No, that probably wouldn't go over very well. I just figured we could try to get him to talk about his relationship with her."

If one had even existed. So far, I'd mostly gotten the impression that he'd been the geeky guy who'd been thrilled to sign her yearbook at all, and that was basically the only connection they'd even had.

Still, sometimes an outsider's perspective could be useful. I'd have to keep my fingers crossed that this trip wouldn't turn out to be a waste of our time.

It took almost exactly two hours to drive to the UNM campus. During that time, Max and I discussed the logistics of me moving in with him, and planned to stop at my place after we got back to Las Vegas.

"You don't have to move everything at once," he said. "But enough that you'd be able to be at the ranch for a week or more. Then we can start slowly moving things in, figuring out how to mix whatever stuff you'd like to bring from your house with the things that are already at the ranch."

That might be a difficult task, since I'd definitely gone for a modern farmhouse vibe when I redecorated the home I inherited from my grandmother, and Max's ranch was much more rustic. However, since I only planned to take over clothes and toiletries at first, I figured I could put off the tough decisions for later on.

"How are we even going to be able to get a week's worth of my stuff out of there if I still have paparazzi camped on my doorstep when we get back?" I asked, knowing I sounded way too plaintive.

Max, as usual, didn't seem at all concerned. "Oh, I figured I'd text Lou when we get closer, let him know what's going on, and then he and Al and Gordon can run interference. It probably won't keep the paps from guessing what we're up to, but at least we won't be tripping over them the whole time."

That seemed like a decent enough plan. We might not be able to completely keep the paparazzi at bay, but at least we could make their lives as difficult as possible.

After that, Max said he thought we might have an early dinner at Campo, the restaurant at the Los Poblanos resort in Albuquerque. Since I'd heard of the place but never been there, I said that sounded like a wonderful idea. Plus, lingering down south for a while might also help with avoiding the photographers currently camped out in my neighborhood, since there was always the hope that they'd tire of hanging around and would disappear to their hotels and Airbnbs after it got dark and I still wasn't home.

With one thing or another, we passed the time until we reached the UNM campus a little before three. It took some time to find a decent parking place near the physics building, but eventually we were able to grab a spot that a perfectly restored MG convertible had just pulled out of.

"Scott Emerson's office is on the second floor," Max told me as we got out of his Bronco.

I nodded and followed him into the lobby. The building was a gorgeous steel and glass structure, very new, very modern, and had obviously been built in the last couple of years. Even though Max had all the intel he probably needed from Al, he still paused by the directory to confirm that information.

"Yep, Room 204," he said. "Let's go."

Rather than wait for the elevator, we took the stairs. With each step, I could feel myself growing more and more tense, even though I tried to tell myself I had nothing to worry about. We were just trying to gather a little information. It wasn't as if this was going to be an interrogation or anything close to it.

Assuming, of course, that Scott Emerson

wouldn't just throw us out of his office as soon as we told him our reason for being there.

I tried to convince myself that wouldn't happen...mostly because, even though I doubted a physics professor would be quite as star-struck as someone like Evelyn Hodge, I had to believe he would still think twice about acting that way toward someone as famous as Max.

At least, I hoped he would.

We reached the second floor. Room 204 was only a few doors down from the stairs, which meant I didn't have a lot of extra time to compose myself.

Then again, maybe that was better. Sometimes the best thing to do was to just jump right into the pool and hope you'd be able to swim.

The door to Scott Emerson's office was open, but Max still didn't walk right in, and instead knocked and said, "Professor Emerson?"

"Come on in," came a man's voice.

The two of us entered the office, which looked about as I'd expected, with bookcases lining the walls and an enormous desk strewn with papers placed a little closer to the window than the door. That desk looked even more crowded because two large flatscreens took up a great deal of the space.

Scott Emerson looked out from behind one of those screens, brows drawing together slightly as he seemed to realize that Max and I weren't just a couple of grad students wandering by. And I had to admit I was surprised to see that, while he still couldn't exactly be called handsome, he'd grown into his gawky features, and now was what you could call interesting-looking, maybe even distinguished, with his long nose and high cheekbones.

"Hi," Max said, moving forward, hand already out. "I'm Max Sullivan, and this is my fiancée, Skye O'Malley."

I'll admit that my cheeks colored just a little bit at that description. It was the first time Max had referred to me as his fiancée in public, and I definitely liked the sound of it.

The professor stared at Max for a moment, something like recognition finally dawning in his hazel eyes. "Aren't you...?"

"Yes," Max said easily, since he'd dealt with this identical situation probably hundreds of times before. "I'm that Max Sullivan."

"My daughter loves your movies," Scott Emerson said, then backed his chair away from his desk so he could stand up.

It wasn't often that someone topped Max's six foot two, but Professor Emerson must have been at least two or three inches taller. No wonder he'd looked so gangly and outsized in that yearbook photo I'd seen of him.

"What can I do for you two?" he asked next, since he'd obviously guessed we were there for a particular reason, and not because we'd just gotten the urge to drop in and discuss particle physics, or whatever his specialty was.

Max gave me the slightest sideways glance, signaling that he thought it was my turn to step in. While I would have liked him to continue to carry the conversation, I knew we were here because I was the one doing most of the work to find Mandy Carson's killer. And I knew I'd keep on doing it even if I had to dodge paparazzi the entire time. I'd made a promise to her, and I wouldn't go back on those words, even if the situation had gotten a lot more complicated over the past couple of days.

"I wanted to ask you about Mandy Carson," I said simply, and Professor Emerson blinked.

"Excuse me?"

"You went to high school together, didn't you?" I asked, and he nodded.

"We were in the same class," he replied, then added dryly, "Although that was the extent of our association."

"You weren't friends?"

Okay, I knew that question was just a little disingenuous, since it was painfully obvious just from looking at her yearbook that the two of them had pretty much nothing to do with one another.

For a moment, he was silent. Then a lopsided smile touched his thin lips, and he shook his head.

"I doubt she knew I existed," he said.

"But she let you sign her yearbook," I pointed out.

Another pause. The professor looked at Max, then back at me, and said, "Why bring this up now?"

"We're trying to figure out what really happened to her," I responded. "Solving murders is kind of a hobby of mine."

I paused there, wondering if Scott Emerson might mention the murder investigation Max had been involved in a year ago. But since he didn't say anything, it seemed clear enough to me that, while he might have a passing acquaintance with Max's movies because of his daughter being a fan, he definitely didn't follow anything that was even close to celebrity gossip.

For the first time, I noticed the plain gold band on Scott's left hand, something that made me oddly pleased. It was always nice to know that someone who definitely hadn't been popular in high school and probably had been the butt of some jokes had still managed to have his own happy ending...probably a lot happier than some of the popular kids who'd looked down on him all those years ago.

"No one knows," Scott said at last. "The police talked to everyone, questioned anyone they even remotely suspected, and they still couldn't come up with any solid leads. As for the yearbook, I heard

Mandy had a goal that year to have everyone in our class sign it—even geeks like me. It definitely wasn't because she cared whether I signed it. I doubt she even remembered my name." He stopped there and shook his head, something that looked like a halfway rueful smile touching his mouth. "I'll admit I had kind of a crush on her, but I suppose that wasn't too strange. Half the guys in our class did, too."

He sounded almost detached as he spoke, as if he was talking about someone else entirely. I supposed that wasn't too strange—clearly, the man who stood in front of Max and me now was a completely different person from who he'd been almost forty years earlier.

Did he remember that he'd written a long, flowery paragraph in her yearbook? I didn't know, and wouldn't ask. All my instincts told me he hadn't killed Mandy, that she'd only been a wistful, passing crush, and definitely not a source of frustrated love culminating in a single act of violence.

"Honestly," Scott went on, "I haven't thought about her in years. It was a tragedy, but...."

He didn't bother to finish the sentence. Obviously, he'd moved on, and there would have been no reason for him to dwell on the girl whose life had been cut short, not when he was busy building a new life of his own.

"Was there anyone else you can think of who

might have been violent if she'd rebuffed them?" Max asked then. "One of the other guys at your school?"

Scott shrugged. "Not really," he replied. "Like I said, a bunch of guys had crushes on Mandy, but it was more a 'worship from afar' kind of thing, if you know what I mean. I'm fairly sure that even if you went and questioned all of them, too, you'd find they were a lot like me—they went on to have their own lives and their own families. High school was a very long time ago."

Somehow, I doubted that many other people from Scott Emerson's graduating class had earned a Ph.D. and were now teaching physics, but I got the point. I was actually engaged to my high school crush...well, Max had also been my grade school and junior high crush...but I knew my situation wasn't all that common. Most people were all too glad to leave high school behind and become the person they aspired to be.

Surprising me, Scott said, "Have you talked to Jeff Hodge?"

Max tilted his head, also apparently caught off-guard by the other man's question. "Not yet," he replied. "But I thought he had a cast-iron alibi—he was off at a football game or something, right?"

"Yes," Scott said. "Estancia, I think." A faint smile touched the corner of his mouth, and he added, "I rarely paid attention to that sort of thing, but people talked about it so much after Mandy's body was found that it just kind of stuck in my head. Anyway, I'm not suggesting Jeff murdered her. I'm only saying he obviously knew her a lot better than I did."

"How long had they been dating when she died?" I asked, realizing that was something Evelyn hadn't mentioned during Max's and my meeting with her.

"A while," Scott responded. "I think they started going out when they were both still in eighth grade. A lot of people I knew thought they were going to get married right after high school, or at least make sure they were going to attend the same college."

Interesting. Mandy hadn't mentioned anything about that, but maybe she'd thought it was sort of a given, that it was the kind of thing everyone knew. I had the impression she lingered on this plane precisely because she was so connected to it, and therefore just assumed I—or anyone else living in the present time—knew what she did.

Max was frowning, and I got the feeling he was trying to puzzle through the same things that were bothering me. "Then didn't people think it was kind of strange that he hooked up with Evelyn so soon after Mandy died?"

Scott ran a hand through his hair, mussing it a little. He'd hung on to what looked like almost all the same sandy hair he'd had in his high school photo, a trait that might have made him the envy of some of his former classmates.

"It wasn't that soon," he said. "Maybe about six months? I don't know. I just remember that people were talking about them going to the prom together, and that was the first time they showed up as a couple to anything. I guess the two of them spent a lot of time together after Mandy died, and they realized they were good together. I really wasn't paying that much attention."

Which made sense—it sounded as if Scott had run in entirely different circles from Mandy and Jeff and Evelyn, so it wasn't as though he would have been paying a lot of attention to their personal lives. However, I noticed he was frowning as he spoke, as if something had bothered him.

Max must have made note of Scott's expression as well, because he asked, "What is it?"

The other man shrugged. I didn't detect anything forced about the gesture, so I assumed he was being honest when he said, "I guess it seemed a little weird to some people, just because Evelyn wasn't Jeff's type. She was actually kind of nerdy— she played the piano...seriously, not just because her parents made her take lessons...and everyone thought she was going to head off to Juilliard or something after she graduated. I think Mandy hung out with her because they'd been friends since first grade, and she didn't want to dump her just because they didn't have much in common anymore."

This was also news to me. Then again, I doubted that Evelyn would have wanted to tell me that she and Mandy shouldn't have really even been friends in high school, considering they didn't have many shared interests.

I thought of Deanne's and my enduring friendship, and how, despite all the things we'd gone through together, we'd never once thought of not being a part of each other's lives. But then, we had a lot in common—we both loved Las Vegas, its history, the people who lived there, all the various ups and downs of life in a small town. True, I was much more into cooking than she was, but we both liked to garden, and to go to the movies when we had time. And even though she probably could have been a member of the in-crowd at school, she'd held herself apart, her loyalty to me not allowing her to hang out with the girls who'd often been openly mean to her best friend.

It sounded as if Mandy had been the same way, and again I thought of how different her specter seemed from the girl the people who'd known her had described. But, as I'd thought only a couple of days ago, being stuck in Plaza Park for nearly four decades was probably enough to make anyone crabby.

"Well, Jeff and Evelyn must have had more in common than anyone thought," I commented. "Since they're still married all these years later."

"Are they?" Scott responded, now looking mildly curious. "I didn't know that. I never bothered to go to any of our high school reunions, so I haven't kept up with anybody. Didn't see the point."

No, I supposed he wouldn't have. People like Scott Emerson just wanted to get the hell out of town and not look back, and I couldn't really say I blamed him.

"Anyway," he went on, "I've got a meeting in ten minutes, so...."

He'd already given us so much excellent information that I couldn't really protest, so I just nodded. "Oh, of course. Max and I will get out of your hair. Thanks for taking the time to talk to us."

"It's no problem," Scott replied. "I hope I helped a little."

"You did," Max told him. "Thanks again for letting us crash your office."

The man smiled, as I'd expected him to—even physics professors weren't immune to my fiancé's effortless charm—and the two of us headed out and back down the stairs.

Once we were outside, Max said, "Well, that was a lot."

"I know," I replied. "I'm positive he had

nothing to do with Mandy's death, but he gave us some good intel."

"All that stuff about Mandy and Jeff," Max remarked, then shook his head. Looking almost sheepish, he added, "I know some people were saying the same thing about me and Raylene, even though I'd known partway through senior year that I was going to end things."

Since Raylene Bryant was safely in our rearview mirror and no one I would ever have to worry about again, I let myself remark, "Seriously? Everyone thought you were the 'it' couple."

That comment got me a grin. We were almost to the car by then, so Max waited until he'd unlocked the Bronco and we'd both climbed inside before he said, "Nope. I was pretty checked out at the end there, but I knew how much Raylene wanted us to be prom queen and king, so I went along with it. I left for college as soon as I could, though."

The very same university we were currently visiting. I had a feeling, though, that Max hadn't spent much time hanging around the physics department.

"Anyway," he continued, "let's get out of here. It's not really dinnertime or lunch, but we can still have a pretty awesome nosh at Campo. Sound good?"

"Sounds perfect," I replied. Because whatever

else happened, I knew I wasn't going to pass up on a chance to hang with Max at a restaurant that had been on my bucket list for a while.

I could only hope Mandy wouldn't mind too much that we were taking some time out for a little fun.

CHAPTER 13

Playing by Ear

Our late afternoon "snack" at Campo was everything I could have hoped for—the most amazing charcuterie board I'd ever experienced, beautiful local wine, and a lemon tart that Max and I shared. We lingered there long enough to watch the setting sun turn the Sandia Mountains a blush pink, the color that had earned them their name, since "*sandia*" meant "watermelon" in Spanish.

It was a little after six by the time we got on the highway, and although there was some residual traffic from the tail end of rush hour, it wasn't enough to slow us down too much. That meant we got to Las Vegas about a quarter after eight. Dark had fallen, and I was glad of that, because it meant if any paparazzi were still hanging out on my street, they might not recognize Max's Bronco until it was too late.

He turned the corner and cruised past my house while I took a quick scan of the neighborhood. "Looks like they're gone," I said, once I realized I could identify every car parked on the street as one belonging to my neighbors. "I guess they really did get bored and leave."

"Sure seems that way," he agreed.

Still, he drove to the end of the block before coming back, as if he wanted to reassure himself that my assessment of the situation had been correct. Once he'd pulled into my driveway, he turned off the engine and shifted so he could look at me.

"Even though they seem to be gone," he said, "we still need to make this fast."

"That's fine," I replied. "I know exactly what to bring. This will only take a couple of minutes."

Those assurances seemed to make him relax slightly, and once we were inside, he waited in the living room, doing his best to peek past the curtains without looking too obvious, while I hurried upstairs to get my things together.

I hadn't been lying when I'd told him I was prepared for this moment. Down from the shelf in my closet came my overnight bag and rolling suitcase—something I'd bought years ago and never actually used—and out of the drawers came four pairs of jeans and six black tops of various sleeves lengths and weights. Throw in some underwear and bras, socks, and sleep shirts…not that I was sure I was going to need those…my toiletries and blow dryer and various assorted hair products, and I figured I was good to go. Worst case, if I'd forgotten something really important, Max could always send Lou or Al over to fetch it for me.

Although I hadn't been timing myself, I guessed that I'd stuck to my five-minute allotment, because Max looked pleased when I reappeared with the overnight bag slung over one shoulder and the rolling suitcase bumping its way down the wooden stairs.

"You were really able to get packed that fast?" he said.

"Of course," I replied, knowing I wore a smile that bordered on smug. "You're surprised?"

"Considering I've dated women who took two hours to pack, yes, I'm surprised…and impressed. But let's get going."

My brain immediately went to all the various women the tabloids had reported Max being with over the years, trying to figure out which one he was talking about. Then I told myself it was silly to think about that, because whoever it had been, she was no longer a part of his life. The important thing was that we were together now, and his past didn't matter.

I allowed him to take the rolling suitcase, mostly so I'd have a free hand to lock the front door behind me. We went to the Bronco and placed the luggage in the cargo area before getting into the front seat.

Not a moment too soon, because just as we were backing out of the driveway, two cars came around the corner, speeding up once they saw Max's SUV leaving the property. Before I could even blink, his foot hit the accelerator, and we practically leaped forward, tires screeching, smoke blowing out from behind us.

I hung on to what Deanne affectionately referred to as the "Jesus handle," praying we wouldn't crash into anyone who'd had the bad luck to come to the nearest intersection at the same time we did. Luckily, it was late enough that most people were home, and we were able to blow through my neighborhood without incident.

However, once we reached 7th Street, he didn't slow down, but just kept going as if all the hounds of hell were behind us.

"There's no one back there," I ventured, but Max didn't take his eyes off the road.

"That doesn't necessarily mean anything," he replied. "They could have called some of their buddies to let them know we were on the move. It's not like there's anywhere we could go except back to my ranch."

True enough. And although under most circumstances I would've had a few choice words to say about going almost thirty miles an hour over the speed limit, right now I figured the best thing to do was just hang on and hope we didn't encounter any cops. Not that Max couldn't afford a speeding ticket, but the last thing we wanted was to get pulled over while trying to maintain a safe distance between us and any pursuing paparazzi.

Luckily, though, it seemed as if the police were busy in other parts of town, or they just weren't patrolling this section of 7th Street. Also, traffic was minimal to nonexistent, so I didn't have to worry about us endangering any innocent bystanders.

When we were about a half mile away from the entrance to the ranch, Max pulled his cell phone out of his pocket. "Call Lou," he told it, and immediately Siri connected the call. "Lou, it's Max. We're coming in hot. Make sure the gate's ready."

"Will do," came through the tiny speaker in the iPhone.

"Thanks."

Max returned the phone to his pocket, while I couldn't help smiling a little. "You really do sound like you're reenacting a scene from one of your movies."

Maybe a corner of his mouth twitched. "True, I might have said that line once or twice. But it works for the situation."

I couldn't dispute that comment, not when we were now bouncing along the gravel lane that led to his property at roughly twice the posted speed limit of twenty-five miles an hour. Good thing his Bronco had been built for this kind of punishment —the going was far from smooth, but I never got the feeling that we were going to lose control and head right over the edge of the road and into a ditch.

And there was the gate up ahead, already open and waiting for us. Lou waved as we sailed through, then pushed the button to have the gate close as soon as we'd cleared it.

Now Max finally slowed down—not to a crawl, but to a speed a little more suited to the driveway. He pulled up to the garage, hit the button for the opener, and pulled inside.

"I'll have Al or Lou go get your car sometime tomorrow," he said, now sounding almost apologetic. "But I just wanted to get us out of there as quickly as possible."

"It's fine," I said, although I still hated the idea of making either one of his security guys have to get up at the crack of dawn to chauffeur me around. "I'm glad we got away."

Now Max finally grinned, blue eyes lighting up in the illumination from the Bronco's dashboard. "Yeah, I'm pretty sure those paparazzi are pissed off right now."

"Serves 'em right," I responded, and Max leaned over and kissed me on the cheek.

"Damn straight. But now, let's get you settled."

It did feel a little strange to follow Max into his bedroom. Of course, I'd been in here before, but now I wouldn't be merely sharing a few hours with him. No, this room was about to become our room.

Good thing I'd always loved the space, loved the simple pine furniture and black iron bedstead, loved the Navajo rug with its earthy shades of red and brown and blue underfoot. Again, it was very different from what I'd chosen for my own house, but that didn't mean I couldn't appreciate its warm charm for what it was.

Not sure exactly what I should say, I put my tops and jeans and underwear in the dresser, noting how Max had made one entire side of the piece available for my belongings.

"There's plenty of room in the closet, too," he said, coming closer. "But I noticed you didn't bring anything that needed to be hung up."

"Oh, I'll get that stuff later on," I told him as I closed a drawer, then turned back around. "But it's nothing I need right away—I mean, unless you plan to take me out for dinner at a five-star restaurant sometime soon."

That was my little joke, since Las Vegas was pretty short on five- or even four-star restaurants. However, his expression was serious enough as he replied, "I'll take you anywhere you want. Dinner in Santa Fe...or Paris, if that's what you'd really like."

A wonderful little thrill went through me. I knew he wasn't making idle boasts. If I really wanted to jump on a plane and have my first dinner at a Michelin-starred restaurant, then he'd do everything in his power to make it happen, including chartering a private jet to land at Las Vegas's small general-aviation airport so it could whisk us away to France.

In a way, it was almost scary to think what someone with his money and resources could accomplish.

"I think we have a murder mystery to solve first," I said.

"No, we have a murder mystery to solve, second," he countered. "Because I have something better in mind for right now."

He bent and touched his mouth to mine, and I eagerly kissed him back.

Yes, we definitely needed to make this room ours...in the best way possible.

"Sorry," I mumbled the next morning as I slid out of bed. I'd really been hoping I'd be able to slip away without waking up Max, but he'd stirred just as soon as I started to move.

"Don't be sorry," he said, and reached over to touch my hand. "I know you have to get up at this ungodly hour. I just didn't want you to leave without a kiss."

He pulled me to him and gave me a very gentle kiss on the lips, one that told me he knew better than to initiate anything when I needed to be at the shop at five-thirty. For about the thousandth time, I realized how thoughtful he was, how unlike his public persona. Most people thought he was a take-charge, macho type, but I knew the real Max Sullivan.

Okay, he'd been pretty take-charge the night before, but that was because he'd been protecting the woman he loved.

It was too bad that I didn't have any time to waste, because it would have been lovely to linger in the bathroom, luxuriating in the full-body jets in the enormous walk-in shower, or to soak in the gorgeous standalone tub that had a place of pride beneath one window. But because I doubted many of my customers would be happy to learn there weren't muffins that morning because I'd stayed playing with a bath bomb for too long, I did my usual quickie shower, glad that I'd washed my hair the morning before and so wouldn't have to waste time on it today.

I'd known that either Lou or Al would be driving me to work today, but I was startled to see both of them hanging out in the kitchen, obviously waiting for me to appear.

"Al's going to take me over to your place after he drops you at the shop," Lou explained. "That way, I'll get your car and park it behind the coffee shop, and it'll be there for you once you're off work."

That seemed like a good plan, even though once again I was assailed by pangs of guilt at making both of them be up so early in the morning. However, I knew any apologies I might make would only be brushed off, so I just thanked them and said I was glad I'd be able to drive myself here to the ranch at the end of the day.

"Oh, you'll be driving your car," Lou said. "But one of us will accompany you. I don't want any of those camera-toting bastards getting anywhere close."

I hadn't really stopped to think about that, but then I realized I was being naïve if I didn't think at least a couple of the paparazzi would try to tail me back to the ranch once I was done with work.

This was really getting ridiculous. Unfortunately, unless one of them became outright threatening, there wasn't much I could do to prevent them from doing their job.

Loathsome as that job might be.

The three of us headed to the garage, where we got into Al's 4Runner and headed out. As usual at that hour of the morning, the streets were nearly empty, and we made good time, arriving at Levitation Latte at five-thirty on the dot.

"See you at three-thirty," Al said as I opened the car door. "Don't even try to leave unless one of us is here."

"I won't," I promised. No, I definitely wouldn't do anything that stupid...and even if I tried, I guessed Gordon would stop me before I had one foot out the door. I sort of doubted any of the photographers would try to physically harm me, but I also couldn't forget that some fairly awful accidents had occurred just because the paparazzi were hot on someone's heels.

At least the alleyway was utterly deserted, empty and dark. As I headed up the back steps, I couldn't help smiling.

Those paparazzi were pretty damn dedicated... but even they didn't want to stake out my coffee shop at five-thirty in the morning.

While I was mixing up that day's batches of muffins and waiting for Deanne to arrive, I couldn't help picking at what Scott Emerson had told us yesterday, how Evelyn and Jeff had seemed to be kind of an odd couple but had ended up together anyway. Had there been any kind of a connection between the two before Mandy had died, or had love only been able to bloom after she was gone?

Hard to say. Then again, maybe there had been a tiny spark, something neither one of them would have acknowledged at the time because they both loved Mandy too much. But after she was no longer a part of their lives, it was possible they'd finally found the courage to realize they were the ones who were truly meant to be together.

Problem was, I didn't know if I dared ask Mandy about any of it. She might have been a ghost for nearly forty years, but her previous life was still fresh in her mind, still felt as if she'd only left it a few days earlier. Trying to question her about her boyfriend's feelings for her best friend might end in disaster.

Then again....

I glanced at the clock. Ten minutes until six. Deanne would be here shortly.

In the meantime, though, the muffins were in the oven, and I had a few minutes to spare.

And I doubted the paparazzi would have come out in force in the last twenty minutes.

That seemed to settle things. I took off my apron, slipped on my jacket, and headed outside. Sure enough, the alley was still empty, and so were the streets around the Plaza. In a little while, the earliest dog walkers would start to come out, but I planned to be safely back inside Levitation Latte before they showed up.

I hurried across the street and into the park, heading for the little clearing that Mandy had made her afterlife home. She must have been expecting me, because as soon as I paused under one of the cottonwood trees, she appeared, standing a few feet away.

"I was wondering when you were going to come back," she said, her annoyed tone seeming to signal that she'd been feeling neglected.

About all I could do was shrug. "I've been trying to follow up on a few things," I told her. "Do you mind if I ask you a couple of questions?"

She raised an eyebrow. "You've already asked me a lot of questions."

"I know," I said. "But now I want to know about Jeff and Evelyn."

At once, Mandy's expression grew stony. It seemed pretty obvious to me that, although she hadn't been able to keep tabs on everything that was happening in Globe, she knew that her former boyfriend and best friend were now together, and had been for a long time.

"What's that thing people always say?" she responded. "'It's time to move on'? Well, Evelyn and Jeff definitely moved on...fast."

"And that upset you?"

Mandy's gray-scale form faded in and out, then seemed to solidify again. Was that one way of showing she was angry? Maybe she had a harder time manifesting when her emotions were all over the place.

"Well, duh. Of course it did." She crossed her arms, and for the first time, I noticed she wore a school ring on her right hand. On the middle finger of her left hand was a small heart set with a diamond.

A promise ring?

"I mean," she went on without pausing, "Jeff and I always said we would be with each other forever. And then only a little more than six months after I died, he goes with Evelyn to the prom? Gag me."

It took a lot of effort for me not to smile at that comment. Most of the time, she really didn't sound like a stereotypical '80s Valley girl—Las Vegas, New Mexico, was a long way from the San Fernando Valley—but in that moment, she could have easily played the lead in some kind of 1980s teen-angst movie.

Well, if it was shot in black and white, that is.

"But Evelyn was your best friend," I pointed out. "Wouldn't you want her to be happy?"

Mandy sent me the kind of look only a teenager could master, the sort that seemed to indicate I had to be the dumbest person on the planet.

"Yeah, I wanted her to be happy, but not with *my* boyfriend!"

Fair enough. Unlike Jeff and Evelyn, Mandy was frozen as she'd been nearly forty years ago, still a sixteen-year-old in mind and body and spirit. It must have been very hard for her to grasp the concept of learning to say goodbye to someone you'd lost and having the strength to start a new chapter in your life.

"Did you ever try to stop them?" I asked then, genuinely curious. "I mean, like you did when you destroyed the marigold mural?"

A second or two passed as Mandy stood there, arms still crossed, mouth now tight. I couldn't say for sure, but it kind of looked to me as though she didn't want to answer that question in case she incriminated herself.

"Maybe," she muttered, and I lifted an eyebrow.

"'Maybe'?" I repeated. "How?"

"I tried going to Evelyn's house and slamming the piano lid on her fingers when she was practicing." This came out in a sulky undertone, as if she knew she needed to reply but really didn't want to.

"That's not very nice," I said, and Mandy shrugged.

"I know. But it didn't work. I mean, I could go to her house and go inside, and it felt like I was touching the piano lid, but nothing happened. It took a long time before I figured out how to do stuff like this."

All around us, the dead leaves that had been lying on the ground swirled up from their resting places, making what looked like a bunch of miniature tornadoes before the energy that was driving their movement stopped and they all drifted to the ground.

"That's impressive," I remarked.

She rolled her eyes. "Whatever. Anyway, I couldn't affect anything around Evelyn, and when I tried to appear to Jeff, to warn him away like I was that ghost in *A Christmas Carol* or something, nothing happened. So, I was just stuck watching them get together. It sucked."

I'll bet. While I definitely didn't approve of some of Mandy's methods, I also couldn't give her too much grief over feeling the way she had.

What would I have done if I were suddenly dead, and I saw Max take up with someone else?

I tried to tell myself that the situations would be completely different, that Max and I were adults, and if I prematurely left this mortal existence, I'd still want him to be happy.

That was a very noble sentiment. Whether the situation would actually play out that way in real life, I had no idea.

"I'm sorry," I replied, because there really wasn't much else I could say.

But I realized time was ticking, and if I lingered in the park for too much longer, I might run afoul of an early-bird paparazzo.

"I'm going to find who did this to you," I said quietly. "I can't get Jeff back for you, but—"

"Like I'd want him now," Mandy cut in, her tone scornful. "He's an old man."

Before I could tell her that being in your early fifties didn't exactly make you "old"—and that even though she was a ghost, technically she was the same age—she disappeared.

All right, then. I couldn't change the past...but I could make damn sure Mandy's killer didn't have a future.

CHAPTER 14

Over–Exposed

D eanne shook her head as I recounted what had gone down the evening before when Max and I came back from our excursion to Albuquerque. "There ought to be a law," she said, hands still busy with refilling one of the napkin dispensers.

Although I'd thought about the same thing, I forced myself to shrug. "I think the paparazzi would claim that violated their First Amendment rights or something. I guess if they stay far enough back, I can't claim assault."

"Still." She set the dispenser back on the counter and reached for the cup of coffee she'd poured for herself a few minutes earlier. "Can't you get a restraining order?"

Good question. I seemed to vaguely recall

hearing that some celebrities had done that very same thing and made a mental note to ask Max about it. It could very well be that our particular batch of photographers hadn't crossed any real lines yet...although I supposed we could reasonably claim that we'd been put in danger by the way we had to race away from my house the night before.

"I can check with Max," I said. "But I have a feeling there isn't much we can do about it right now except try to make ourselves as inaccessible as possible."

Which wouldn't be super-hard, now that I was staying at the ranch. I'd still need to go back to the house to pick up a few things here and there, but I'd brought enough that I wouldn't have to make such a trip for a while. And who knows? Maybe by then the paparazzi would have gotten weary of playing hide-and-seek with Max and me and would have left to seek other, more accessible victims.

That was probably a vain hope, but I refused to give up on it.

Deanne made a disgusted sound, but she obviously could tell I didn't want to talk about it anymore, and instead asked if we'd found out anything interesting during our trip to Albuquerque.

"I'm not sure," I said. "I mean, I learned a few things about Mandy and Evelyn and Jeff, but I still don't feel like I'm getting the whole picture."

In fact, I felt as though I was missing some vital piece of information, which was generally what happened when I was trying to figure out a murder and had collected a lot of interesting bits and pieces that didn't quite fit into a coherent whole. But I tried to tell myself that, since this wasn't the first time I'd tried to solve a mystery, I'd get a better grasp on things with time.

Time I wasn't sure I had, considering how grouchy Mandy had been when I'd talked to her only an hour ago. She'd told me she would hold off on wreaking any more destruction until I had a chance to continue working on the investigation, but I couldn't quite shake the impression that she was all too ready to let loose if I took too long.

"You'll figure it out," Deanne said, with the supreme confidence of someone who wasn't carrying this particular burden. "You always do."

Maybe I shrugged. However, I didn't have a chance to reply, because Lucy Margolis came bustling into the shop, what looked like a newspaper clutched in one hand. She waved it at me, saying, "Have you seen this?"

Mystified, I shook my head. Yes, I got the weekly Las Vegas *Herald,* but I doubted there could be anything in our local paper that would have gotten Lucy quite so stirred up.

She thrust the paper at me. "Look."

I took it from her and laid it on the counter. At

once, I could see what she was talking about, and my heart sank.

The paper she'd handed me was the latest edition of the *National Inquisitor,* and right there on the front page was the screaming headline, "Max Sullivan Hooks Hometown Hottie!", accompanied by a photo of Max and me shielding our faces as we hurried out of Smoky Joe's.

It definitely didn't look as if the *Inquisitor* had wasted any time publishing those photos it had taken a couple of nights ago.

"Well, at least they called you a 'hottie,'" Deanne said with a grin as she looked over my shoulder to inspect the paper.

Somehow, that wasn't very reassuring. "I think they were just going for the alliteration," I replied. The photo could have been worse, I supposed, but at the same time, it wasn't very flattering, either. I wore the proverbial deer-in-the-headlights look— not so surprising, considering I'd had what felt like a hundred flashes going off in my face at once—and Max wore the appearance of someone who could have cheerfully socked every single one of those photographers right in the nose. In general, his tabloid photos looked a lot more relaxed than that, but I guessed when the photo had been taken, he was only worried about trying to protect me.

Lucy, on the other hand, appeared positively

indignant. "I hate that they can follow people around like this when you're just trying to live your life."

"I know," I said wearily. "That's why we have Gordon watching the shop—so they can't come in here and try to take pictures of me while I'm foaming a latte, or whatever." I spared a glance toward the door, where Gordon Shaw was keeping guard. He'd shown up at ten 'til seven, just as he had the day before, and I had no doubt that he'd be there tomorrow, too, and for however long all this nonsense lasted. "But thanks for showing me the paper," I added, since I knew Lucy had only been trying to watch my back. "At least now I know not to react if I see it when I'm in the checkout line at Walmart."

If I'd even be allowed to engage in such a mundane activity. True, Max had been shopping in town for months, and these days, hardly anyone batted an eye when they ran into him, but that was because the paparazzi had gotten bored and long since given up on Las Vegas. Now, though, they had some fresh meat in the form of Max's new fiancée, and I doubted they were going to give up so easily.

Lucy seemed a little deflated by my low-key response to her revelation, but really, what was I supposed to do? I couldn't allow myself to be angry and annoyed all the time, or I'd never get anything done.

She folded the paper and stuck it in her over-sized purse, although something about the set of her mouth told me she would have been all too happy to toss it into the nearest trash can. "Well, I just thought you should know."

"And now I do," I said calmly. "Can I get you a latte?"

To my relief, the flow of customers picked up that day, as if everyone had realized that Gordon was now at least a semi-permanent fixture, and they didn't want to deprive themselves of their caffeine fixes just because an intimidating individual was now standing guard at the door.

Kyle came in not too long after Lucy's visit and we chatted for a bit, although I could tell he was just trying to pass the time and didn't have much of any import to discuss. He'd given Gordon some side-eye as he walked in, but he didn't ask any questions, telling me he'd already heard through the town grapevine exactly why I'd had to hire a security guard.

And then, a little after two, Cathy Newman walked in.

She was a regular, although she only visited the coffee shop a couple of times a week, and not every day the way some of my customers did. I'd been hoping she would make an appearance, since I knew that would be the only way for me to pick her brain without looking way too suspicious. If I'd tried to go talk to her at her house, she would have known something was up.

Of course, the second I started asking questions about Mandy Carson, Cathy would probably realize I wasn't just making idle chitchat.

I'd sent a significant glance at Deanne, signaling to her that I wanted to be the one to take Cathy's order. Being my best friend, she understood that look immediately and made sure she was busy refilling one of the cinnamon shakers as the other woman approached the counter.

"Your usual?" I asked. Some of my customers liked to mix things up, but Cathy always had a latte with extra foam no matter the time of day or what the weather might be like outside.

"Yes, please," she replied, just like she always did.

I went over and poured some coffee into a mug, then heated the milk and swirled it in, finishing with an autumn-leaf pattern on top. While I worked, my mind raced as I tried to figure out the best way to casually mention Mandy Carson without sounding like I was asking any leading questions.

To my infinite relief—and surprise—Cathy was the one to bring up that subject.

"I saw your *ofrenda* for Mandy," she said. Like Evelyn, she'd aged well, and appeared a lot younger than the fifty-four or so I knew she had to be. Maybe her blonde hair was being helped along a good bit at this point, but her blue eyes had very few lines around them, and she still looked as if she was a size six at the very most. "It was really beautiful. But...why?"

A valid enough question, I supposed, especially considering that I hadn't even heard of Mandy before a week ago. However, I'd already thought of the best way to approach this particular problem, and hoped my answer would sound logical enough.

"Well, after dealing with those ghosts at the Plaza Hotel, I started wondering if there were any other mysterious deaths or unsolved murders in Las Vegas," I explained. "That was how I found out about Mandy and how she died. It was sad... and scary. So, I just thought it would be nice to make an *ofrenda* for her at the Day of the Dead event."

Cathy's expression was both sad and sympathetic, as if I was the one who'd lost a friend and not her. "It was really awful," she said. "Even all these years later, I think about her, think about what kind of life she'd have if she were still with us."

I doubted I could have asked for a better opening than that. "Do you think she would have still been with Jeff?"

For just a second, Cathy looked surprised, as if she hadn't expected I would have known such an intimate detail about her long-dead friend. But then she relaxed and said, "Evelyn told me you and Max Sullivan came to talk to her."

Now it was my turn to be a little startled, although I realized immediately afterward that it wasn't so surprising for Cathy and Evelyn to have kept in touch. They'd both stayed in Las Vegas, after all, and hadn't moved away and lost track of one another.

Some of my confusion must have shown on my face, though, because Cathy said, now smiling a little, "Evelyn just had to let me know how she'd gotten a visit from Max, of all people. She was completely star-struck. And then she told me why you talked to her." A slight pause, during which her smile faded. "It was really nice of you to make that *ofrenda.* I suppose one of us should have thought of doing that once the Day of the Dead festival was announced, but we lost Mandy so long ago...."

Cathy's words trailed off there, but I thought I understood. It wasn't that she or any of Mandy's friends didn't care, but she'd died so many years earlier, and no doubt most—if not all of them—had suffered their own losses over the course of those decades.

"It's all right," I said. "I'm glad I could do it for her." I hesitated, then knew I needed to plow ahead, even if some of the things I wanted to ask might have sounded rude. "Did it...did it surprise you when Jeff and Evelyn got together?"

Once again, Cathy looked startled, as if she wasn't sure why I would care about something like that. But then she replied, "Well, I guess so, mostly because neither of them had shown any interest in the other person before then, and...just between you and me...Evelyn really didn't seem to be his type."

"But Jeff was Evelyn's type?" I inquired.

Now Cathy just smiled. "I think Jeff was most people's type, just like Mandy was the girl a lot of guys had crushes on. That's why everyone thought they were such a dream couple, like they were meant to be together. But yes, Jeff was a really good-looking guy back in the day. Even so, I never saw Evelyn make eyes at him or flirt with him or do anything like that. She had her own boyfriends, although she never seemed to date anyone for very long. But even if she hadn't been dating people, she loved Mandy way too much to make a move on her best friend's boyfriend."

So much for that. It really did sound as if Evelyn and Jeff had gradually grown into being a couple, drawn together by their mutual feelings of loss and grief.

"Did you have any theories as to who could have killed Mandy?" I asked next, and immediately, Cathy shook her head.

"No," she said. "I mean, it was all any of us could talk about for a while, but we could never find any solid answers. Most of the kids at school decided it must have been a vagrant, someone passing through town who'd committed an awful act of violence before disappearing. I mean, the police would have figured it out if it was someone who lived here."

One would think. And I thought I understood the impulse to blame someone outside the community, a person who had absolutely no connection to the town. That was a whole heck of a lot easier than making yourself believe a neighbor or a friend could have done such a horrible thing.

"Yes, I suppose they would have," I said, although I had my own doubts. Our local police force was really good in a lot of ways, but a crack FBI-trained forensic team they were not.

I didn't mention any of that, though. It was pretty obvious to me that Cathy had lived for years with the belief that a stranger had killed her friend, and I didn't see the point in trying to disabuse her of the notion now. Maybe she'd be forced to accept an uncomfortable truth if I really did manage to find out who Mandy's murderer really was...or maybe not.

And honestly, I couldn't say for sure that Cathy and others who shared the same belief weren't correct in thinking it had been someone just passing through who'd killed Mandy Carson. If that was the case, then I knew I'd probably never be able to track them down.

Depressing thought. Mandy wouldn't like that a single bit.

Cathy paid me for her drink and left, and Deanne came over, expression questioning.

"I'm not sure if that helped very much," I said. "It really does sound as if Evelyn and Jeff Hodge just naturally got together. Nothing to see here."

Being Deanne, she didn't seem too discouraged by those words. It took a lot to get my best friend down. "I don't know," she replied. "You've talked to a lot of people, but you've never talked to Jeff himself. Maybe it's time to hear what he has to say."

I wanted to argue that I didn't know what that would prove, but I stopped myself. Deanne was right. He'd been the person closest to Mandy, so it only made sense for me to at least try to speak with him.

Problem was, I had no idea where he even

worked. I knew I needed to meet with him some-place away from his home, because otherwise, Evelyn would think I didn't trust what she'd told me and was trying to get information behind her back.

Okay, that was pretty much exactly what I was doing, but still. This wasn't even about thinking that any of them were guilty. No, it was just me desperately trying to gather as much information as I could in the hope that some-thing would stand out and point me in the right direction.

"Do you know where he works?" I asked, knowing the question was probably futile but figuring I should try, anyway.

As I'd thought, Deanne shook her head. "No, I'd never even heard of the guy before you mentioned him," she said. "I don't think he's ever come in here, or even if he did, it wasn't a regular thing."

The same for me. I definitely didn't have all thirteen thousand and some-odd residents of Las Vegas memorized, and it wasn't as though every single person who lived here frequented my coffee shop.

Luckily, I had my own resources.

I texted Max and told him what I was looking for, and he sent back a reply and let me know he was going to tell Al what I was looking for, and to hang tight for a little bit. Sure enough, only five minutes later, another text came through.

Jeff Hodge is a systems administrator at New Mexico Highlands University. His office is on the third floor of the main administration building.

Perfect. Somehow, I had a hard time envisioning the former captain of the football team as an IT guy, but I had to admit it was a smart field for him to go into if he wanted to stay in his hometown and still make decent money. Unfortunately, the vast majority of the jobs here in Las Vegas were entry-level retail and food service positions, necessary but not exactly what you could call high-paying.

Thanks, I love you!

Anytime. Want me to come along?

I hesitated. As much as I loved Max and loved having him with me as much as I could, he was awfully conspicuous. It was one thing for him to accompany me to Albuquerque to NMU so we could talk to Scott Emerson. I had a feeling it was something else entirely to show up at Jeff Hodge's office here in town. If I went by myself, no one would pay any attention to me, or at most, might think I was one of the university's students.

Probably better if you don't. But I'll be home as soon as I can...I'm going to stop at Jeff's office on the way to the ranch.

Okay. I'll let Lou know.

Which meant Lou would be driving with me, running interference. Probably a good thing—I had a feeling Jeff Hodge would feel even less compelled to talk to me if I had a horde of paparazzi on my tail.

If he talked at all. Well, I'd find out one way or another in a few hours.

CHAPTER 15

Unchained Melody

New Mexico Highlands University was almost walking distance from my coffee shop—not that I planned to go anywhere on foot, not when I had all those celebrity photographers just waiting to pounce and get some juicy images of Max Sullivan's fiancée looking tired and frazzled after a day at work.

No, I went in the bathroom and combed my hair, applied fresh lip gloss, and then waited for the text letting me know that Lou was waiting for me out back. Deanne and I finished closing up, I checked Tilly's bowls to make sure she had both food and water, and then my phone pinged.

I'm here.

That was all the text said...not that I'd expected much more. Lou was a man of few words.

"Okay, Lou's here," I told Deanne, who'd just

gotten her purse out of the cubby where she kept it during the workday. "I'm heading over to see Jeff Hodge."

"Good luck!" she replied.

I was definitely going to need it.

After setting the alarm, I hurried outside. Lou had parked his big Toyota Tundra behind my Crosstrek and Deanne's RAV4—mostly to make sure none of the photographers lurking a few yards away could get close enough to do the same thing. Knowing I probably would have an audience, I'd already put on my sunglasses and had my key fob out, and was able to get into my vehicle without exposing myself too much. Deanne did much the same thing, and as soon as we were both in our cars and had them started, Lou backed up his truck so we'd be able to get out...and would have a straight shot down the alley.

Seeming to know it would help if she ran interference, Deanne pulled out first while I fell in behind her. That way, she and Lou formed a barrier of sorts, something the paparazzi would have a hard time penetrating.

The ploy seemed to work, because we were able to exit the alley without anyone trying to stop us. We stayed in that formation until we reached the university, where I pulled into the visitor parking lot while Deanne kept going south on Bridge Street so she could pick up Grand Avenue.

Lou, on the other hand, continued to follow me. The parking lot was still fairly crowded, but I cruised around until I could find two spots next to each other, since I knew my borrowed bodyguard wouldn't be too thrilled if I ditched him.

It didn't look as if anyone had followed us here, but I still waited until he got out of his truck and came over to the driver's side of my Subaru.

"I'm going to the administration building," I told him after I also exited my vehicle and locked the doors. "This is going to be kind of a private conversation, though."

"Sure," Lou said easily. "I'll just wait for you in the hallway outside the guy's office."

I probably should have known there was no way I could have gotten Lou to stay in the parking lot. Trying not to sigh, I said, "Okay. But please try not to be too conspicuous. I don't want this guy to clam up."

"He'll never even know I was there," Lou promised me.

I had my doubts on that score—Lou weighed about 250 pounds, was somewhere in his late forties, and looked like he should be hanging out on the set of *The Sopranos* or something, not waiting in a hallway at New Mexico Highlands University.

But because I realized this was the best he was

going to offer, I only nodded and said, "Okay. This way."

Although I'd never gone to school here, I knew the campus well enough because I'd helped my grandmother cater a couple of events here back when I was helping her with The Tea Spot, which had been Levitation Latte's name when she still owned the shop. In those days, it had been more of an actual restaurant, with sandwiches and desserts to go along with all the various teas she offered, and occasionally she'd be asked to provide catered snacks at symposiums and other special events.

Anyway, I headed straight for the administration building, Lou at my heels, and went over to the elevators. Normally, I would have used the stairs, but I had a feeling my companion wouldn't have appreciated having to exert himself quite that much.

Things seemed pretty quiet on that Tuesday afternoon, and no one seemed to pay us any particular attention. When we got to the third floor, I paused to glance at the directory helpfully mounted on the wall by the elevator, and determined that Jeff Hodge occupied office number eleven.

Lou said, "I can wait here. It doesn't look like we were followed, so I think it's safe."

Thank God. Yes, he'd told me he would try to be inconspicuous, but loitering outside Jeff's office would have made Lou stick out like the proverbial sore thumb.

"Perfect," I replied. "I'm not sure how long this is going to take, but I doubt it's going to be more than twenty minutes at the most."

"Not a problem," Lou said, and pulled his phone out of his pocket. "I can find something to amuse myself."

I nodded, then headed down the hallway toward Jeff Hodge's office. When I got there, the door was open, so I paused awkwardly in the opening, then ventured, "Mr. Hodge?"

He looked up from where he sat behind a big metal and wood desk. At once, I was struck by the thought that geeky Scott Emerson had aged a lot better than Las Vegas High's former football star. The thick brown hair I'd seen in Jeff Hodge's yearbook portrait was now thin and mostly gray, and even though he was sitting down, I could tell he'd put on a lot of weight and had quite a large paunch.

However, his smile was friendly enough, if a bit puzzled. "Can I help you?"

I wasn't too surprised that he looked confused. After all, his was the kind of job that probably didn't involve much interacting with people who weren't coworkers, and while I probably could have passed for a student at the university, I definitely wasn't anyone he would have interacted with previously.

Although he hadn't given me a direct invitation, I went ahead and entered his office. "My name is Skye O'Malley. I was hoping you would talk to me about Mandy Carson."

Now his expression seemed even more bewildered. I got the distinct impression that Evelyn hadn't said anything about my visit to their house, maybe because she hadn't thought it was worth mentioning to her husband...or maybe because Mandy was still an uncomfortable topic between the two of them and she hadn't wanted to bring it up.

"'Mandy'?" Jeff repeated, as if he wanted to make sure he'd heard me correctly. "Um...why?"

Clearly, he didn't know who I was, or that I was Las Vegas's supposed ghost-whisperer. I still wasn't sure I could lay claim to that title, despite my recent success with getting Ana Moreno's restless spirit to move on to the next plane of existence.

That was probably a good thing. Only Max and Deanne knew I'd been speaking to Mandy's spirit, and I wanted to keep it that way.

"Oh, trying to figure out cold cases is a hobby of mine," I said, which wasn't an outright lie. "I was doing some research and found out about Mandy, so I thought I'd talk to the people who were closest to her."

Jeff's expression didn't change. If he'd ever harbored any guilt about moving on to a relationship with Evelyn only six months after his high school sweetheart was murdered, it definitely didn't show in his face now.

"I'm not sure I have anything to tell you that's not already in the police records," he said slowly. He still looked more bemused than anything. "I was at the game in Estancia when it happened."

"Did Mandy tell you about her plans to stay here in Las Vegas so she could study?"

He gave a small nod. "Sure," he replied. "Usually, she would have been there with the squad to cheer us on, but she told me her parents were going to freak out if she got a D in history, so she told me she couldn't make it that night. I wished she could have come to the game, but our plan was to go to UNM together, and she wouldn't have been able to do that if she didn't keep her grades up."

Throughout his little speech, I kept watching him carefully, but I didn't see anything in his face other than maybe a little wistfulness, as though he was thinking if only she'd decided to blow off going to the library that night so long ago, his life might have turned out very differently.

And although I'd been harboring some hopes that maybe the whole football game story wouldn't hold up, I realized now that was just silly. His alibi wasn't something you could easily fake—it wasn't as if he'd claimed to have gone to the movies with a friend, or hung out at someone's house playing video games. No, he'd gone and participated in a very public sporting event that had probably been attended by hundreds of people. There was no way to pretend something like that.

"When I found out," he went on, then paused, as if, even after all these years, he needed to steady himself when talking about his murdered girl-friend, "I was so mad at myself."

"At yourself?" I repeated, not sure what he was driving at. "Why? You didn't have anything to do with what happened to Mandy."

At least, I was pretty sure he didn't.

"Because I wasn't doing that great in U.S. history, either, and she tried to get me to stay here and go study with her at the library," Jeff replied. "I told her I couldn't, that it was a huge game and I couldn't just skip out on the rest of my teammates. So I left. But if I'd listened to her and been more worried about my grades, she'd still be alive today."

How was I supposed to respond to that state-ment? It seemed fairly clear to me that Jeff Hodge must have been beating himself up all these years, even though absolutely no one could have imag-ined what was going to happen to Mandy that night.

"Do you think you'd still be with her if she'd lived?" I asked, genuinely curious. After all, most high school couples didn't survive much past graduation. People changed so much once they were free to make their own lives.

I'd changed, and so had Max. For us, though, it was more that the people we'd grown into were the ones who were meant to be together, not who we'd been back in school.

Would it have been the same way for Jeff and Mandy?

This time, he was silent for so long that I wasn't sure whether or not he was going to answer me. Maybe he was thinking of his life with Evelyn, and if he answered yes to my question, then that would have been a betrayal of their marriage.

There weren't any family pictures on his desk, only a single photo of the two of them together, a picture taken someplace with palm trees in the background while they beamed at the camera. Jeff had more hair in that picture, which made me think it had probably been taken a while back. They looked happy, but what did that mean? Pictures never told the whole truth.

I realized that I also hadn't seen any photos at their home that seemed to show they'd had children. True, some people weren't that into having family pictures all over the place, but usually there were at least a couple. If they'd had kids, they would have been grown and out on their own by now, possibly had started their own families.

Well, maybe it was just the two of them. Not everyone had a burning desire to have children, or maybe they'd struggled with infertility.

Somehow, that thought made the whole situation even sadder.

When Jeff finally spoke, it was in barely a murmur. "I don't know. I just don't know."

Lou gave me a curious look when I met up with him by the elevator. "Did you learn anything?"

I didn't know how much Max had told him. Probably not a lot, just that we were trying to solve an old case, something that seemed prosaic enough when you didn't mention that the chief instigator of the investigation was the murdered girl herself.

Because I wasn't quite sure what to make of my conversation with Jeff Hodge, about all I could do was give a helpless lift of my shoulders. "I'm not sure. I mean, now I'm pretty positive he's innocent, but hearing what he had to say was still sad."

"Unsolved cases suck," Lou agreed as he pressed the button to summon the elevator. "But you seem to be pretty good at this kind of stuff. I'm sure you'll figure it out."

That was just about the same kind of reassurance I would have gotten from Max. I tried not to smile, since I could tell Lou was being serious.

All the same, it would be good to get back to the ranch and have Max give me a reassuring hug.

I could use one about now.

———

We talked about the case over dinner, and Max only shook his head when I related what Jeff had told me about the night Mandy died.

"That's rough," he said. "I mean, the guy clearly had nothing to do with any of this. And to still feel guilty so many years after the fact...." He shook his head, then reached for his glass of cabernet. I'd done steaks in his *sous vide* machine that night because they were quick and easy, but I was finding I didn't have much of an appetite. "It sounds like everyone involved should have gotten a lot of therapy to deal with their feelings about Mandy's death."

Yes, they probably should have. Unfortunately, mental health professionals weren't exactly thick on the ground in Las Vegas even now, and I had to believe things hadn't been much better back in the 1980s.

I made a sound of assent and drank some of my wine. "Anyway," I said, "I keep eliminating people, but I don't feel any closer to finding any real answers. Maybe I won't. Maybe Mandy will just turn into a vengeful spirit and go crazy on the town until we all leave."

Max looked like he was doing his best to hide a smile, based on the twitch I detected at a corner of his mouth. "I don't think the situation is quite that dire," he told me. "But maybe it's time for you to consult the tea leaves again."

That didn't sound like a very good plan to me, even though I'd brought all my supplies with me just in case I got desperate enough to try another reading. "The first one didn't work so well," I replied. "I'm still trying to figure out why a key is supposed to be important in this case."

"Maybe Mandy left her house key at the library and was heading back to get it?"

On the surface, that theory made some sense... except for the part where her parents had been home at the time of the murder, and all she would have had to do was knock to be let in. "I don't think so," I said, knowing how dubious I sounded. "There wouldn't have been any reason to go back, especially because she left as the library was closing. There wouldn't have been anyone there to help her. Also, the key came up when I asked who was responsible for her murder, not why it happened."

Max absorbed all this, frowning slightly, but since he didn't try to argue with any of the points I'd made, I knew he'd realized his suggestion was off base. "Still," he said, "sometimes you've gotten weird readings at first, and then had a follow-up that clarified things. It couldn't hurt."

Okay, that was fair enough. It was true that sometimes a second reading provided additional clarification...just as sometimes all I got was the exact same results, as if the tea leaves were trying to tell me they'd already provided the pertinent information and didn't see any reason to give anything else to go on.

"Well, I'll have to try after work tomorrow," I said. "Evening readings never go very well, especially after I've had something to drink. And I'm too rushed in the morning to do the ritual—my head needs to be as clear as possible."

"That makes sense," Max responded. "And I'm sure Mandy isn't going to begrudge you another day. She knows you're working as hard as you can."

I didn't know whether I was as confident on that point as my fiancé. The teenage specter had seemed particularly cranky when I spoke to her early this morning, although that could have been because we'd been talking about Jeff and Evelyn, clearly a sore point with her.

But since I really couldn't do anything more than what I'd already been doing, I didn't argue.

No, I only nodded and picked up my knife and fork, knowing I needed to finish my steak before it got too cold.

Maybe the coming day would give me a new outlook on the situation.

It still felt a little strange to lie down in the big king-size bed I now shared with Max, and to realize this was where I would spend all my nights from now on...well, unless he decided we should jet off to Tokyo or something.

Tonight he seemed to understand I only wanted to snuggle, to curl up next to him and feel the warmth of his body, hear his breathing grow slower and more rhythmic as he slipped into sleep. It took me a little longer to drift away, probably because I still wasn't used to sleeping here. Soon enough, though, my eyes closed, and I fell into darkness.

Only to find myself standing in a large garden with wide green lawns and perfectly manicured hedges. It definitely wasn't the glade I imagined when communicating on the astral plane—that was a wild place, beautiful, of course, but nothing like the orderly beauty I saw around me now.

In fact, it felt oddly familiar, although I couldn't think of where I'd seen it before. Off in the distance was a huge white building with a large cupola on its roof, the flag mounted there flying in a stiff wind. Again, it felt like something I'd seen before, although I couldn't say where. All I knew was that there was nothing like it anywhere in Las Vegas, New Mexico, or any place around here.

A ripple of gentle piano music washed over the scene, a melody I thought I knew, even though I couldn't say how, or from where. It, like the scene in front of me, had the feel of a memory despite my not having any idea exactly where it was.

Just like that, the dream faded away. I rolled over, still half asleep, and let it go. If it was important, its significance would, with any luck, become clear at some point.

For now, though, I was content to slide back into slumber and hope that the next day would bring me some answers.

CHAPTER 16

Rhapsody on a Theme

T he dream didn't fade with the coming of morning, though. In fact, it floated in my mind, as vibrant as it had been while I slept the night before. I had no idea what it was supposed to mean...but I also knew my strange O'Malley gifts were probably at it again, doing their best to send me signals I was too clumsy to interpret.

However, being haunted by the image of that grand white house—or whatever it was—definitely wasn't enough to keep me from heading to work the next morning, this time with Al playing escort, his Toyota 4Runner close enough on my heels that I doubted anyone would try to insert themselves between us.

No one made the attempt, though, and I made it to the coffee shop without incident. The streets were dark and quiet as they always were, and it definitely felt to me as though the paparazzi had decided it wasn't worth giving up a few precious hours of sleep just to catch me going through the back door of Levitation latte.

Or maybe they really were gone.

I didn't see any sign of Tilly, which didn't surprise me too much. Sometimes she was here when I came in to work, and sometimes she was already out roaming around, seeing if there were any good early-morning morsels to rummage from one of the dumpsters in the alley.

Her food bowl was empty, though, so I refilled it and got her fresh water as well. Those tasks managed, I got started on that morning's muffins and pastries, and had everything in full swing by the time Deanne showed up.

"It's quiet out there," she told me as she put on her apron. "I came down Bridge Street just so I could see if anyone was still camped near the shop, but I didn't see anyone."

Had my wishes really come true? Had all those photographers decided I was way too boring to stalk, and gone back to L.A. or wherever else it was that they'd come from?

I told myself not to get my hopes up. Most likely, they knew there wasn't much chance of seeing me until we were open for business, so there wasn't any point in loitering nearby this early in the morning.

"Good to know," I replied. "Maybe we'll be able to send Gordon home."

"You really think he'd leave?"

About all I could do was smile. "I doubt it."

She went out front to tidy up and get the first batches of coffee going, then came back to the kitchen, where I'd just popped some blueberry and maple bacon muffins in the oven. "Did Jeff Hodge have anything good to tell you?"

"Not really," I said. "I can tell he's still kind of torn up about Mandy, even after all this time, but he just told me the same stuff I already knew. So, I really am starting to think the killer must have been a stranger, because no one here in Las Vegas seems to know a single damn thing about what happened that night."

"Unless they're lying," Deanne responded. "I mean, would you be able to tell if they were?"

Not being psychic, I doubted it. Sure, Calum McRae had said I was psychic, that I definitely had talents most other people didn't possess, but I still didn't really believe him. To me, being psychic meant being able to read people's minds, and I definitely couldn't do anything close to that. The best I could manage was trying to read someone's body language and hope I wasn't way off base.

"No," I said. "But even if one of the people I've talked to was lying to my face—and lying to everyone else in their life—do you really think they would have been able to maintain that lie for so many years?"

A weighted second or two passed, and then Deanne shook her head. "Probably not," she said, speaking slowly, as if she didn't enjoy having to admit to such a thing. "I mean, I suppose someone could, but not anyone who was still living here in Las Vegas. People are way too much in each other's business."

That was for sure. I loved my hometown, but news and innuendo traveled awfully fast here. I didn't see how anyone could keep such a terrible secret for so many years in that kind of environment. If they'd moved away, sure. That was an entirely different situation.

Unfortunately, there was no way in the world I could ever track down everyone who'd left Las Vegas to put down roots somewhere else, so if the killer wasn't here, I was definitely out of luck.

"Which means I have nothing to go on," I said, and sighed. "And Mandy isn't going to wait forever for me to get my act together."

"It won't take forever," Deanne assured me. "You just need more time."

And that was something I wasn't sure I had. Plaza Park's resident ghost was being quiescent for now, but I really didn't know how long that particular state of affairs would last.

For now, though, I needed to concentrate on

opening the shop for the day...and hope inspiration would strike sooner rather than later.

Business was almost back to normal that Wednesday, and I was all too glad for it. Yes, I always liked feeling that the coffee shop was doing well...although I'd already realized that any money worries were now a thing of the past, thanks to my engagement to Max Sullivan...but my relief mostly stemmed from knowing that if I was being kept busy, then I wouldn't have much spare time for brooding over Mandy's murder case.

Three-thirty rolled around, and, while I was happy to head back to the ranch—and also glad that Lou was accompanying me this time, because the paparazzi had reappeared as soon as the shop opened at seven—I still couldn't ignore the feeling that I was missing a vital piece of the puzzle, that the dream I'd had the night before was something more than just a beautiful image accompanied by some pretty music.

Max greeted me with a kiss. As usual, he looked relaxed and happy—as he should, since he'd spent the day with his horses and puttering around the house, and not having to do anything in particular. All right, that wasn't exactly true, since I knew he had some scripts he was reading and a couple of

Zoom calls set for earlier in the afternoon. Still, it wasn't what anyone could have called a demanding schedule.

"Is it okay if I have the kitchen to myself for a little while?" I asked. "It's hard for me to concentrate on a reading when someone else is around."

"Take as long as you need," he replied. "I'll go back to one of my scripts...although I can already tell it's a clunker. I don't know what Margaret was thinking, sending me something like that."

"She was probably imagining an eight-figure payday for you," I said, and his expression turned slightly pained.

"Maybe, but I'd rather have that same payday with a decent script."

I chuckled, and he kissed me again before heading down the hall to his office. The house was big enough that it had two offices in addition to its complement of four bedrooms, and I knew Max was expecting me to take over the second office. It was barely furnished, had only a desk and a chair and not much else, and I was looking forward to being able to decorate it and make it mine, even if I probably wouldn't end up using it very much.

First things first, though.

The antique teacup and matching saucer I used for all my tea-leaf readings had already been given a place of honor on a shelf in one of the kitchen cupboards, so I got them down and set them on the granite countertop, then used the pot filler to add water to the kettle. That made the task so much easier and faster, and I wished I'd had the budget to install one when I'd remodeled my house a few years ago.

Not that it mattered now, since it didn't look as though I'd be using that kitchen for much anymore.

I pushed the thought away, along with any lingering concerns about my timeline for moving in with Max. So what if we'd accelerated things a bit? We'd both known I'd eventually end up here… and besides, I had to admit to myself that this kitchen blew mine out of the water. There was no way in the world I could have afforded a ten-thousand-dollar stove, or a custom range hood, or any of the other high-end finishes in the space.

And now that I had all those wonderful toys to work with, cooking in here would be a breeze.

The gunpowder green tea had been tucked away in the walk-in pantry, so I got it out now while I waited for the water to boil. Soon enough, everything was ready to go, and I poured the water over the tea, once again holding that same thorny question in my mind.

Who really killed Mandy Carson?

A moment to sit with the tea, to let that question settle even as the tea leaves began to float in the steaming water. A few more minutes to wait for it to cool enough for me to drink, and then I took my first swallow.

This was the part of reading tea leaves that always felt interminable; mostly, I just wanted to drink all the tea so I could get on to the actual work. However, impatience was pretty much antithetical to divination, since the whole point was to relax and allow yourself to be open to whatever messages the universe was trying to send you.

So that was why I made myself drink slowly and calmly, my mind as quiet as I could make it, racing thoughts pushed aside as best I could so they wouldn't crowd out the important stuff. All my focus needed to be directed to that one question, the thorny problem of the identity of Mandy's killer.

Eventually, the tea was gone, the teacup tipped upside down so the last few drops of liquid could spill onto the matching saucer. I turned the cup right-side up, then peered inside.

All the residue had clumped in the bottom in one large, indistinguishable blob...except for two leaves stuck to the side in a rounded, asymmetrical form that took my brain a few seconds to recognize.

Was that a grand piano?

Without the legs, obviously—the tea leaves had formed a shape that was pretty clearly a piano as viewed from above.

Well, if Mandy Carson had been killed by a falling grand piano like some character out of a Bugs Bunny cartoon, this reading might have made more sense.

Except....

I thought of the piano I'd seen in Jeff and Evelyn Hodge's home. True, it had been a small spinet tucked against the wall and not a concert Steinway, but....

Was it possible that I'd misread Jeff? Had he somehow managed to make everyone think he'd been at the football game when in fact he was back in Las Vegas, lying in wait because he knew his girlfriend would be walking through Plaza Park a little after nine on that cold October evening?

But then a chill went through me.

Jeff didn't play the piano...but Evelyn did.

No way. It wasn't possible.

Or...was it?

That's crazy, I told myself. *Why in the world would Evelyn want to kill her best friend?*

Because she wanted Jeff for herself, a cold, logical part of my brain told me. *She would have known Mandy was going to the library that night, and would have been able to intercept her on her way home.*

Okay, even assuming that was what had happened, would Evelyn really have had the physical strength to throttle Mandy Carson?

I'd noticed during our meeting that Evelyn was a large woman. Not fat, but with a big frame, and several inches taller than I was, almost five ten. If Mandy's ghost was the same size she'd been when she was alive, then she had only been around five foot four, maybe even a little shorter. Evelyn's hands probably would have been large enough to wrap around her friend's throat.

Then, with almost an audible *click*, my dream of the night before fell into place. That big white building I'd seen was the Grand Hotel on Mackinac Island, the setting of *Somewhere in Time*, one of my grandmother's favorite movies. And the music in the background?

Rachmaninoff's *Rhapsody on a Theme by Paganini*, a piece that had figured prominently in the film. I remembered how my grandmother had talked about the music, had told me that Rachmaninoff had had famously large hands, and wrote music that sometimes was difficult for people with smaller hands to play, since they couldn't get their fingers to manage those octave-plus reaches.

A chill shivered its way down my spine as I realized that Evelyn, whose hands matched the rest of her frame, would be able to play Rachmaninoff's works with no problem.

This all made perfect sense to me, but I knew I was going to need more concrete evidence to support my theory that Evelyn Hodge was the killer the police hadn't been able to find all those years ago. Of course they couldn't have discovered who it really was. No one in the world would have suspected a sixteen-year-old girl of committing such a heinous crime, particularly when her best friend was the victim.

Mind churning, I took the teacup and saucer over to the sink and rinsed them out, then left them on the counter to dry. Usually, I'd get out a towel to finish the process, but I still didn't know where Max kept everything in his kitchen. I cooked dinner for him all the time...at my house. When I came over here, he either barbecued, or Lou handled the food prep.

Hopefully, that wouldn't turn out to be a problem. I liked Lou a lot and thought his cooking was wonderful, but I also wanted the chance to make this kitchen my own.

I headed down the hall to Max's office, then paused by the entrance. He had his head down, a printed script on the desk in front of him, so I knocked softly on the doorframe.

He looked up at once, expression expectant. "Did you see anything?"

Boy, did I. "Yes," I replied. "I saw a piano. You know who plays the piano? Evelyn Hodge."

Max didn't even blink. "You think Evelyn murdered Mandy?"

"I think so," I said. "I don't have any actual

evidence, but she would have known Mandy was going to the library that night."

"Okay," he said. His head tilted slightly, and he added one all-important word. "Why?"

"Jeff," I said shortly, and a knowing gleam entered my fiancé's eyes.

"Jealousy," he remarked. "It's often a great motivator. So...what's next?"

"I know this sounds silly," I said, "but I really wish I could see Evelyn playing the piano. This theory is based on her having hands that were strong enough to strangle Mandy. If I could see her in action...."

Max didn't look too startled by my unusual request. "That might be easier than you think," he said. "Didn't she mention that she plays piano at the Baptist church?"

"She did," I replied. "So...you think there might be a video of her playing somewhere?"

"Let's look on YouTube," he suggested. "These days, lots of churches put their services and concerts online for people who aren't able to attend services in person."

That sounded like a great idea. I waited for Max to get up from his desk, and then together we headed for the family room, where a huge eighty-inch TV dominated one wall. After making ourselves comfortable on the couch, he reached for the Apple TV remote and turned on the device, then navigated to YouTube and its search option.

Sure enough, First Baptist Church of Las Vegas had its own channel. More than that, it had a playlist of all the concerts Evelyn Hodge had given there.

"Looks like she does more than just play at Sunday services," I commented.

"They probably use the concerts as fundraisers," Max said. "Churches are always looking for ways to raise more money."

I couldn't really argue with that. Instead, I scanned the videos on the playlist and then smiled. "That one," I said. "'An Evening With Rachmaninoff.'"

A minute later, the same strains of "Rhapsody on a Theme by Paganini" drifted out of the built-in Bose speakers overhead.

"I heard that song in my dream last night," I told Max. "At first, I didn't understand what it meant. But then when I saw the piano in the tea leaves a few minutes ago, I got it. Evelyn was a dedicated pianist even back in high school, and that means her hands and fingers would have been a lot stronger and more limber than those of most girls her age. The police probably never thought a sixteen-year-old girl could do something like that, but...."

No point in finishing the sentence. I was pretty

sure Max could visualize the terrible scene just as easily as I could.

"Okay, so we've got a motive," he said after a brief pause. "What do we do now? Go to the police?"

That would have been the easiest way to handle all this. Problem was, while Marie DeVargas was certainly a competent police chief, she didn't have a lot of imagination. I didn't want to think what her reaction would be if I went to her and told her I knew without a shadow of a doubt that Evelyn Hodge had murdered Mandy Carson all those years ago.

After all, my dreams and my tea leaves had told me the truth of the matter, as I realized now that the key I'd seen in my first reading had been the leaves trying to convey the idea of a piano key to me. An actual piano key would have looked like a rectangle and nothing more, so the tea leaves had provided a more metaphorical alternative. Unfortunately, I hadn't been sharp-witted enough to pick up on the clue.

At any rate, speaking with Chief DeVargas and letting her know how the leaves and my dream had guided me to the real killer would probably go over about as well as a death metal song at a church revival meeting.

"No," I said slowly. "We need to get Evelyn to

confess, and we need to record it." I stopped there. "Is that even allowed?"

"It is in New Mexico," Max responded, his tone now much more cheerful. "All you need is the consent of one person, not everyone involved. And since we obviously consent, then it's not a problem."

"Perfect," I said, then glanced over at the clock on the mantel. It was now a little after four, but I didn't think Evelyn would be home from work yet. "We should probably wait a little, though. Maybe go over around five-fifteen?"

"I suppose that'll work," Max said. Now his tone seemed to tell me he thought delaying the confrontation would be horribly anti-climactic, but I didn't know what else to do. There didn't seem to be much point in driving all the way over there, only to find Evelyn was still out.

Besides, I had a feeling this particular confrontation would still arrive a lot sooner than I would have liked it to....

CHAPTER 17

Dead Girl's Party

A nd that hour passed...eventually...so at a
little after five, Max and I got in his Bronco
and drove all the way across town to the ranchette
where Jeff and Evelyn Hodge had lived for decades.
When we pulled onto the gravel drive at just a hair
before five-thirty, though, I blinked in surprise.

There were two cars parked in front of the
garage—a Toyota Camry and a Buick Rendezvous
—and not the single vehicle I'd been expecting.

"Jeff must have gotten home early," Max said,
probably recalling how he hadn't been at the house
during our previous visit here, which had taken
place around the same time.

I wasn't sure what to do about that. In my
mind, I'd imagined the two of us confronting
Evelyn by herself, and I didn't know how having
Jeff there might complicate the situation.

On the other hand, he deserved to know the truth about his life...and the lie he'd been living all these years.

"Well, we'll deal with it," I said. "Ready to record?"

"Just a sec."

He pulled his iPhone out of his breast pocket, then went to the Notes app and started the voice recording function. Back at the house, we'd both agreed that it would be better if he handled this part of the operation—he'd used that function on his phone plenty of times, while I'd never had any need of it, and also, we'd tested it to make sure that our voices would be picked up better when they were muffled by only a single layer of cloth rather than being buried in my purse somewhere.

I was just fine with letting Max walk in front of me and having him reach out to ring the doorbell. He seemed his usual calm, confident self, as if he did this sort of thing every day, while my heart felt as if it was pounding loud enough for anyone nearby to hear.

Jeff was the one to open the door. Astonishment registered on his face when he realized an honest-to-God movie star was standing on the porch...astonishment that only increased when he noticed me standing at Max's side.

"Ms. O'Malley?" he managed.

"Hi," Max said cheerfully. "I don't think we've been introduced. I'm Max Sullivan."

And he extended a hand, one that Jeff Hodge shook in a somewhat bemused way.

"Do you mind if we come in for a minute?" Max went on. "We have something we need to talk to you and Evelyn about."

"Um...sure," Jeff replied, obviously still at a complete loss. "Come inside."

We followed him into the living room. From the kitchen came the familiar sound of a food processor whirring, and I couldn't help giving an inward wince. It sure sounded as though we'd dropped by just as Evelyn was beginning to make dinner.

Max had clearly picked up on the same thing, because I noticed how he sent a quick glance in that direction before saying, "Could you have your wife come in here? This sort of concerns both of you."

"She just started making dinner—" Jeff began.

"We really need to talk to both of you," I cut in, but gently. My entire being dreaded what we were about to say to him, and yet I knew this needed to be done if Mandy was going to have any kind of peace.

Jeff looked as if he wanted to offer an additional protest. He must have thought better of it, though—maybe it was the expressions on our faces

—because he only said, "Go ahead and sit down. We'll be out in a minute."

"Thank you," I replied.

Max and I made our way over to the couch and sat. He took my hand and gave it a little squeeze, just enough to provide the reassurance I definitely needed right then. As he let go, Jeff and Evelyn entered the living room. She looked almost as mystified as he did, but a certain tension in her stance seemed to signal she'd realized this was a little more than a simple friendly visit.

"So," she said, as she and her husband took their seats in the pair of club chairs that faced the couch, "what's all this about?"

A very small sideways glance from Max, as though asking permission for him to speak first. I was more than fine with that plan, so I tilted my head slightly in his direction, letting him know it was okay to lead the discussion.

"How many hours a day did you practice piano when you were in high school?" he asked.

Most people would have considered that question to have come directly out of left field. However, I thought I knew exactly where he was going with this, so I sat there in silence as I waited for Evelyn to respond.

Judging by the air of utter confusion that surrounded her, it was clear she had no idea what he was talking about. "Why does that matter?" she responded.

"Just curious," Max said with a smile.

He definitely knew how to use that smile to devastating effect. And when the recipient already had a massive crush on him....

"I practiced three hours a day during the week," Evelyn said, a note of pride in her voice. "An hour in the morning, and then two after I got home from school. On the weekend, it was more like four hours each day."

A low whistle escaped Max's lips. "That's a lot of practicing."

"It was," she acknowledged. "But I had dreams of being a concert pianist back then. These days, I'm happy to play for my church."

In the chair next to her, Jeff shifted, almost restless, as if he'd heard all this before and knew that asking about Evelyn's practice regime back in high school wasn't the real reason we'd come here.

She seemed to be of the same mind as her husband, because her eyes narrowed then, and she asked, "But what does the way I practiced back in high school have to do with anything? I definitely don't practice that much these days."

"It's because I got to thinking," I said, knowing by the way Max had hesitated that he needed me to pick up the thread here. It wasn't anything I wanted to do, but since it had been my dreams and my tea-leaf readings that had brought us here, it just made sense for me to answer her question. "I've been looking into Mandy's murder, trying to figure out if there was something everyone else had missed back then. And then I started wondering if they'd had a blind spot, had never considered that the person who'd killed her might have been a woman."

Evelyn went very stiff then, while next to her, Jeff seemed to go utterly still, as though he somehow could guess where all this was going but didn't want to acknowledge such a terrible fact.

"Well, a girl, actually," I went on. "Someone her own age, someone who knew her better than anyone else."

"This is ridiculous," Evelyn said then, her tone icy, and made a movement as if to get up from her chair. "I think you'd better leave."

Surprisingly, her husband said, "No, I want to hear what she has to say," even as he laid a hand on her arm, keeping her from rising any further.

I sent him a grateful look for the intervention and continued. "Most girls wouldn't have been able to strangle Mandy, because they would have been around her same size and she would have been able to put up a fight, even when surprised from behind like she was. But you, Evelyn—you were a tall girl back then, just like you're a tall woman today. And your hands and fingers were extra strong from all that practicing."

"I am not going to sit here and listen to this," Evelyn snapped, again attempting to get up from her chair.

However, Jeff's fingers wrapped around her wrist even more tightly, and he kept her from rising more than a couple of inches. "We are going to listen," he said, his voice cold. "We're going to listen to every word."

I wanted to hug him for such an unexpected show of bravery, but instead I went back to my story. "You were jealous of Mandy," I told Evelyn. "She was pretty and popular, and dating the boy you wanted. You knew she only stayed friends with you out of loyalty, and not because she really wanted to keep hanging out with you. So you started scheming how to get rid of her, and when she said she was going to skip the football game and stay here in town so she could study, you figured that was the perfect time to make your move."

Once again, Evelyn shifted in her seat, but the narrow-eyed glare her husband shot at her seemed to indicate he was all too willing to use bodily force if she tried to get away.

"It was cold that night, wasn't it?" Max said then, picking up the narrative. "You were wearing gloves while you were waiting for Mandy in the park. That was why the cops couldn't find any physical evidence. And when it was done, you went home as if nothing had happened. How did you manage that, anyway?"

Face stony, Evelyn retorted, "This whole thing is a total fabrication. In fact, I've got a good mind to sue you both for slander."

Max only stared back at her, expression almost amused. "You sure you want to do something like that, Ms. Hodge? Because I can afford some pretty good lawyers."

Before she could reply, the front door banged open, and an icy wind blew through the room. All of us startled...although I had a good idea who had just arrived.

"You *bitch!*" Mandy screamed.

The songbook that had been sitting open on the piano flew into the air and smacked right into Evelyn's head. She let out a screech and started waving her arms at it, looking for all the world like someone getting attacked by a swarm of bees.

"Stop it!" she spat out, glaring at Max and me.

"Oh, this isn't a Hollywood trick," I said, realizing that while I could see Mandy's gray-scale, ghostly form, no one else around me could. "It's your old friend Mandy. Looks like she's a little pissed off to discover that her bestie was the one who murdered her all those years ago."

"Mandy?" Jeff said, getting up from his chair and looking around wildly. "She's here?"

"Yes," I replied.

"Where?"

"Right in front of you," Mandy said, and Jeff went stock still, even as the flying songbook continued with its mission of destruction.

"You're there," he breathed, and reached out a hand.

Of course, it went right through her, but despite that, it seemed to me that she was now visible to him. Exactly how that had happened, I'd have to figure out later.

Mandy wore an unexpected smile. "You got fat."

"I did," he said, smiling back at her, not embarrassed at all by her pithy...if not very polite...observation. "I didn't have you around to keep me in line."

"Stop talking to the air and help me!" Evelyn cried, hands grabbing for the songbook, which seemed just about as elusive as a fly that didn't want to get swatted.

"Oh, shut up," Mandy said. The songbook dropped to the floor, and she stared at her erstwhile friend. "You killed me just so you could have him."

Now Evelyn went stark white, the blush she wore standing out against suddenly pale cheeks. Next to me, Max said, "wow" under his breath, and I guessed he was now also able to see our spectral visitor.

"I'm sorry," Evelyn said, tone jittery, completely unlike the cool, composed speech she'd exhibited just a few moments earlier. "I just—you had *everything*. I wanted something of what you had. I knew he'd never leave you for me, but with you gone, I had a fighting chance."

"All that time," Jeff said, voice so tight, I was surprised the words were even able to leave his lips. "All that time, you pretended to be heartbroken. You pretended to be helping me with my grief."

"I wasn't pretending about that part!" Evelyn cried, tears beginning to run down her cheeks. "I loved you. I wanted to help you." A pause, and she said in a much smaller voice, "I wanted to help you forget her."

"Well, I never did," Jeff returned. His gaze moved toward the spot where Mandy stood a few feet away. She gave him an encouraging smile, and he added, tone hard, dismissive, "I want you to know you were always second best, Evelyn."

And as Evelyn stood there, tears staining her face, he reached out a hand to Mandy. She clung to it for a moment, smile still steady, and then she faded away, and he was left holding empty air.

"She's gone," I said quietly. "You gave her the peace she needed, Jeff."

His own eyes were suspiciously bright, but he only nodded. "That's something, I guess." He looked over at his wife, who continued to sob, and told her, "I'm going to hire an attorney. You need to do the same thing...although for an entirely different reason."

And Max got his phone out of his pocket, shut off the voice recorder, and said, "I think I'd better call the police."

"All's well that ends well," Deanne said, as she and Mike and Max and I all clinked our glasses together.

I wasn't so sure about that. Yes, I'd found Mandy's murderer, but the truth I'd uncovered had destroyed a marriage.

A marriage built on a foundation of lies, I supposed, but still....

"She's really moved on?" Mike asked. His expression was just the faintest bit skeptical, although he knew better than to question me directly about my ghost-whispering abilities when he had his wife sitting right next to him.

"I'm pretty sure she has," I replied, then sipped some more of my pinot noir. We'd all met at Smoky Joe's so I could tell Deanne and Mike what had gone down at the Hodges' home earlier that evening, and, as I'd expected, they'd been spellbound by the story. "Max and I went by her spot in the park on our way over here, and I didn't see her...and she didn't come when I called to her."

It was more than the lack of a response, though. The other times I'd gone to meet Mandy, I could sense her presence there in that secluded spot between the trees. The air had felt heavy, telling me something was nearby. Now, though...now it just felt like every other place in the park, although one weighted with difficult, painful memories.

Max had handed over his phone to Kyle, who'd been one of the deputies to arrive on the scene. "Take what you need from it, and then let me know when I can have it back," he'd said, and Kyle, looking mystified, had dropped the phone into an evidence baggie.

None of us knew exactly when Evelyn Hodge would be arraigned, but I had a feeling the D.A. would be on it first thing in the morning.

"Well, of course Mandy would move on," Deanne said. "Skye found the person who murdered her. She didn't have any reason to hang around after that."

"I'm not sure that's it," Max countered, and my friend lifted an eyebrow. "I think it's what Jeff said to her."

I nodded, knowing where he was going with this. "He told her he'd never forgotten her, that he'd always loved her. In the end, that's what really mattered to her. And that was why she was able to let go."

To move on to the next plane of this existence, a plane where, I hoped, she would live a much longer and happier life.

Who knows? Maybe Jeff would join her there...someday.

———

"Thank you for doing this," I told Max, who stood next to me, his fingers entwined with mine.

"It's the least I could do," he said, looking vaguely embarrassed. "You made it sound as if Mandy was irritated that no one had put a plaque here."

The wind swirled around us, cold, promising snow overnight if the forecasts held. In the dry yellow grass beneath one of the cottonwood trees had been placed a bronze plaque that said simply, *Mandy Elizabeth Carson, May 8th, 1968-October 30th, 1985. Rest in Peace.*

Almost as soon as Max had sent the request to the mayor's office—promising that he would pay for the plaque and its installation—the approval had come back. By then, the town was swirling with the story, with the realization that a woman who'd lived among them and been a neighbor, friend, acquaintance...wife...had been hiding a terrible secret for all those years.

Jeff Hodge had already filed for divorce, and Evelyn was being held without bail, awaiting a trial that had been set for right after the first of the year. She continued to proclaim her innocence, but because she'd basically come out and said she'd murdered her best friend—and we'd captured that confession on Max's phone—no one believed her.

I looked around the sheltered little spot where Max and I stood, thinking that even though Mandy had moved on, she might have returned now for a moment or two, if only to see her beloved plaque before she returned to her new existence.

But she didn't appear, and the wind was icy on this early day in December. It seemed Mandy really had achieved the peace that had been denied her all those years, and it was now time for Max and me to look forward to our own future.

"Come on," I said, and squeezed his gloved hand.

"Let's go home."

Max and Skye's story will conclude in *Wedding Cakes and Wishes*, releasing in January 2024.

Also by Christine Pope

THE DJINN WARS

(Paranormal Romance)

Chosen

Taken

Fallen

Broken

Forsaken

Forbidden

Awoken

Illuminated

Stolen

Forgotten

Driven

Unspoken

Hidden (March 2024)

———

FAMILIAR SPIRITS

(Cozy Mystery/Paranormal Romance)

Spells and Spaniels

Cauldrons and Cats

Hexes and Hedgehogs

Charms and Chihuahuas (April 2024)

LATTES AND LEVITATION

(Cozy Mystery/Paranormal Romance)

Caffeine Before Curses

Muffins After Magic

Pastries and Prophecies

Eclairs and Ectoplasm

Sugar Skulls and Specters

Wedding Cakes and Wishes

HEDGEWITCH FOR HIRE

(Cozy Mystery/Paranormal Romance)

Grave Mistake

Social Medium

Household Demons

Perpetual Potion

Jingle Spells

Wandering Monsters

Uninvited Ghosts

Prophet Motive

Ballroom Bits

Spell Check

Brew Confessions (February 2024)

———

UNEXPECTED MAGIC*

(Urban Fantasy/Paranormal Romance)

Found Objects

Finders, Keepers

Lost and Found

Finding Destiny

———

THE WITCHES OF WHEELER PARK*

(Paranormal Romance)

Storm Born

Thunder Road

Winds of Change

Mind Games

A Wheeler Park Christmas

Blood Ties

Healing Hands

Wishful Thinking

Smoke and Mirrors

MISS PRIMM'S ACADEMY FOR WAYWARD
WITCHES*

(Fantasy/Academy Romance)

Misspelled

Dispelled

Expelled

PROJECT DEMON HUNTERS*

(Paranormal Romance)

Unquiet Souls

Unbound Spirits

Unholy Ground

Unseen Voices

Unmarked Graves

Unbroken Vows

THE DEVIL YOU KNOW*

(Paranormal Romance)

Sympathy for the Devil

Charmed, I'm Sure

A Wing and a Prayer

Wish Upon a Star

THE WITCHES OF CANYON ROAD*

(Paranormal Romance)

Hidden Gifts

Darker Paths

Mysterious Ways

A Canyon Road Christmas

Demon Born

An Ill Wind

Higher Ground

Haunted Hearts

THE WITCHES OF CLEOPATRA HILL*

(Paranormal Romance)

Darkangel

Darknight

Darkmoon

Sympathetic Magic

Protector

Spellbound

A Cleopatra Hill Christmas

Impractical Magic

Strange Magic

The Arrangement

Defender

Bad Blood

Deep Magic

Darktide

THE WATCHERS TRILOGY*

(Paranormal Romance)

Falling Dark

Dead of Night

Rising Dawn

THE SEDONA FILES*

(Paranormal/Science Fiction Romance)

Bad Vibrations

Desert Hearts

Angel Fire

Star Crossed

Falling Angels

Enemy Mine

———

TALES OF THE LATTER KINGDOMS*

(Fantasy Romance)

All Fall Down

Dragon Rose

Binding Spell

Ashes of Roses

One Thousand Nights

Threads of Gold

The Wolf of Harrow Hall

Moon Dance

The Song of the Thrush

———

THE GAIAN CONSORTIUM SERIES*

(Science Fiction Romance)

Beast (free prequel novella)

Blood Will Tell

Breath of Life

The Gaia Gambit

The Mandala Maneuver

The Titan Trap

The Zhore Deception

The Refugee Ruse

STANDALONE TITLES

Hearts on Fire (Paranormal Romance)

Taking Dictation (Contemporary Romance)

Golden Heart (Gaslight Fantasy Romance)

Night Music: A Modern Reimagining of The Phantom
of the Opera (Contemporary Romance)

Ghost Dance: A Sequel to Gaston Leroux's The
Phantom of the Opera (Historical Mystery/Romance)

Flight Before Christmas (Fantasy Romance)

* Indicates a completed series

About the Author

USA Today bestselling author Christine Pope has been writing stories ever since she commandeered her family's Smith-Corona typewriter back in grade school. Her work includes paranormal romance, fantasy romance, and science fiction/space opera romance. She makes her home in New Mexico.

Don't miss out on any of Christine's new releases —sign up for her newsletter today!

Christine Pope on the Web:
www.christinepope.com